JASON & ANNA LEE
by
Sue Gavin

TATE PUBLISHING
AND ENTERPRISES, LLC

Jason and Anna Lee
Copyright © 2015 by Sue Gavin. All rights reserved.

No part of this publication may be reproduced, stored in a retrieval system or transmitted in any way by any means, electronic, mechanical, photocopy, recording or otherwise without the prior permission of the author except as provided by USA copyright law.

The opinions expressed by the author are not necessarily those of Tate Publishing, LLC.

Published by Tate Publishing & Enterprises, LLC
127 E. Trade Center Terrace | Mustang, Oklahoma 73064 USA
1.888.361.9473 | www.tatepublishing.com

Tate Publishing is committed to excellence in the publishing industry. The company reflects the philosophy established by the founders, based on Psalm 68:11,
"The Lord gave the word and great was the company of those who published it."

Book design copyright © 2015 by Tate Publishing, LLC. All rights reserved.

Published in the United States of America

ISBN: 978-1-63306-852-0
1. Fiction/Literary
2. Fiction/Christian/General
14.11.11

A story of love, that tenacious weed, and the strange places where it grows "....... Behold, I make all things new." Rev. 21-5

DEDICATION: To my Betsy, a light in the forest, a glow in my heart.

ACKNOWLEDGMENTS: First of all, to the God of my understanding, without Whom nothing is possible. Then to Alice Gavin, Betty Lawrence, Joan Dunn, Lydia Boone, Connie Brown, and Doris Gidcum, because they could hear my song before I could sing it; to Frank Grady and Howard Schwartz, who showed me things I didn't know were there; to Carol Kittles and Martha Doty, who held me up when I would have fallen; Chuck Miller, Dean Hiza and Harmon Woods - they know damned well why; and finally, my dear friend Jan Wilson, who has tolerated untold amounts of nonsense from me.

JASON & ANNA LEE

Chapter One

1:00 a.m., January 29th, 1997 The street lamp made a halo around Jason Anglethwaite's bright blond head; small ice drops from the sleet glittered in his hair, sliding down on to the upturned collar of his windbreaker. His thin shoulders were hunched against the wind, chin close to his chest, hands jammed into his pockets. He just stood there, under the light, looking at the toes of his sneakers.

The downtown streets were deserted at this hour of the night, buildings blind-eyed and unblinking against the muted glow of the street lamps that made the icy air a prism. It seemed to Jason that he was on an unknown planet whose inhabitants had abandoned it long ago in favor of more hospitable surroundings. Like locusts, they had left behind only the brittle shells of their existence, old buildings that housed scavengers, perhaps, floors termite-eaten, with that smell that comes with rotting wood.

Jason was standing in the middle of the old garment/shoe district of downtown St. Louis, which had seen better days. While there was still a thriving trade in the daytime, it was not nearly what it had been, and some of the older buildings had been abandoned; some for sale or lease, and the loneliness was ubiquitous, almost palpable. The only living creatures to be found were the night scavengers and sleeping street people. And to see any of these, one had to look very hard.

Anna Lee Macintosh hefted her impressive bulk onto an elbow to get a better look at what she thought might be an angel standing there under the streetlight. The glitter of the sleet, the bright gold of his hair, looked other-worldly to Anna Lee's alcohol-soaked brain, and she silently swore that never, no NEVER again would she stoop to drinking canned heat. No, sir, that shit'll make you blind and crazy before it finally kills you. She only did it any way to shut up poor old Willie the Wino, always bawlin' and squallin' that nobody'd drink with him. Hell, if he'd just wipe the snot off his nose once in a while maybe you could stand to talk to 'im and be around 'im.

Slowly, the mist in her head broke up and she realized that she was not hallucinating (although God knows, she sure shoulda been), the apparition she was seeing was real. That led to the next astonishing fact that her overtaxed mind was trying to process: here was a beautiful white boy, eleven, maybe twelve years old, standing on a deserted downtown street in January, and it was probably about two o'clock in the morning. Her worst fear was confirmed when he raised his hand to wipe a stray cold drop that had fallen from his bangs onto his nose.

"Ssst, boy, c'mere, get on over here, boy," her loud whisper caused poor old Willie the Wino to scratch and mumble in his sleep. Jason looked up, peered into the alley, and, unable to see Anna Lee, resumed meditating his shoes.

Anna Lee sat straight up and began waving her hands. "Look here, boy, over this way," as she waved her hand. "Damnation," she mumbled, pulling herself up on one elbow "I fought too hard for this place by the grate and I'm not gonna leave it." Raising her voice, she said, "Here, boy, here, in the alley."

Poor old Willie the Wino was stimulated to noisy flatulence, twisting in his MD-20/20 coma, as if the sound would lead Jason in the right direction. Jason stooped down a little and squinted into the shadows of the alley. Slowly, he began to make out shapes: a dumpster with a skewed lid and gathered around an air turnaround were several large lumps of indeterminate nature. Bags full of trash? One of the lumps was very animated, seemed to be waving an arm.

Jason moved closer and Anna Lee said, "What you doin' out here, white boy? Where's your mama?" She leaned her broad back against the wall of the building, and propped a foot on poor old Willie the Wino's rump; Willie's snoring continued uninterrupted.

"I just, I," Jason faltered and Anna Lee looked hard at him. She began to see the thin jacket and shabby sneakers.

She spread her large arms, opening up the Army surplus Arctic coat and said, "You come here, boy. You come here to Anna Lee. We'll talk about all this in the mornin'. For now, you just warm up and rest here with Anna Lee."

Anna Lee Macintosh had once stood six feet tall in her bare feet. Even now, having shrunk from time and self-abuse down to five foot eleven, she was still a visual epic. However, in her youth, she was not only highly visible, but a positive delight to see. Anna Lee had grown up in the home of her grandmother in north St. Louis. Her mother had once told her that Art Tatum was her daddy, and she should never be ashamed. Whether or not there were ever any papers to prove that assertion, the fact was that Anna Lee had been heir to somebody's prodigious musical talent, and since both her mother and grandmother were practically tone-deaf, she assumed it was her father. If it wasn't Art Tatum, it didn't matter, because she certainly had musical vision, supported by extremely long fingers. She liked to say that if

Art Tatum was her daddy, then Scott Joplin must have been her uncle, because she had Tatum's harmonic vision and Joplin's hands, the best of both. Joplin, who had likewise been for a time a St. Louisan, had had a dexterity that was legendary.

By the time she was twenty-three years old, Anna Lee had the world by the tail (or as much as a black woman in the U.S. could have in 1958). She was a statuesque black beauty, who sang like an angel and played her piano like it was another body part. By 1960 she was a major attraction in a St. Louis tourist area known as Gaslight Square. Five nights a week, she kept Nick the Greek's Cafe in the AAA listings with jazz that was a credit to Heaven. There was no conversation while Anna Lee performed. Tuesday through Saturday nights, promptly at nine p.m., the waiters stopped serving and the busboys became very quiet in their duties. Anna Lee would stride through the dimly lit room, six feet tall, head high, a smile for the tables she passed on her way to the piano. The piano sat in a little corner with a blue baby spotlight on it. Anna Lee would sit down, adjust her skirt, the bench, perhaps riffle a little through the music, and then strike a chord. The chord would become a riff while she decided what she would do, and then she would proceed to do it. She usually started off with something that swung light and easy, her touch on the ivories equally light and easy. Softly, full of fun, the joy of the music taking her away, Anna Lee would be off and running. Her voice had a lot of range, and she had diligently practiced vocal exercises to develop resonance and breath control, just as she had her scales on the piano. The timbre could be husky, moody, then rich and commanding, by turns. Around about eleven o'clock, when everybody was a little mellower with music and liquor, Anna Lee went into what she called her "Frank Sinatra" mode. She would solicit requests from the house, picking only the softer, more romantic or torchier ones. By one a.m., when it was time to close, the remaining patrons and Anna Lee were all swimming in a state of happy, music-induced hypnosis.

Nobody knows how long this would have gone on or how far Anna Lee's career could have soared, because slowly, imperceptibly, her own body chemistry turned on her and became her enemy. The music that was constantly in her head got loud, loud enough to drown out conversation. At first, it was infrequent, but then people began to notice that in the middle of talking, Anna Lee would suddenly disappear inside of herself, frowning, listening to something that could be heard by no one else.

Her long fingers would draw into fists, and her eyes become desperate. At first, she would look wildly around, and scream, "Turn that damned radio down. A person can't think." When she realized that she was the only one privy to this aural event, she stopped talking about it, but her whole demeanor would turn to one of panic, and for a time, she was lost to the real world. This behavior started to cause problems at Nick's, so much so that a couple of times the owner, Mr. Horace Kapandopoulos himself, spoke to her.

However, there came the time when it ceased to be a problem, because it went beyond solving. Anna Lee lived in a four-family flat on Delmar, a quiet sedate neighborhood which still had a significant Jewish population. All the apartment buildings in this area were of an age, having been built in the twenties and thirties, and their construction was designed to withstand the Apocalypse. Whatever the tenants were doing, their neighbors were seldom privy to it. However, one Saturday afternoon in her flat, Anna Lee slipped away, never to return. The noise in her head started, so dissonant, so loud, that she knew she either had to shut it down, or kill herself. She hunted around until she identified the source, and, armed with a large boning knife, went across the hall to Mr. Jackson's flat.

Mr. Jackson was a retired janitor, widowed, and a long-time resident of the building. He had been on speaking terms with Anna Lee since she had moved in a few years back. He would see her occasionally when they happened to meet in the hall, coming, going, or taking trash out. While he never made any mention of it, he enjoyed her music, her cheery disposition, her beauty. His only son lived in Los Angeles with his family. A quiet man, early on he had learned that the less attention he attracted in this white man's world, the better off he was. Let Rosa Parks defy bus drivers, Dr. King march all over the south, he personally would keep his nose clean, and racial equality be damned. He had some savings, some stocks, some government bonds and a small pension. He wanted to bequeath something to his boy and then leave this world in peace.

This day, a Saturday, when Anna Lee hammered on his door, screeching obscenities, jerked him out of the pleasant reverie he always slipped into while watching the sports shows, particularly fishing. He loved to fish, the calm serenity of watching the lake bubble as the fish moved around in it was sometimes even more enjoyable than an actual catch. A small man, he opened his door and looked up into Anna Lee's maniacal eyes, saw the knife, and instantly slammed it shut. His amazement at her behavior was equaled only by his fear. Enraged, Anna Lee kicked at the door and, lapsing into black street lingo, yelled, "Jackson, you turn that motherfuckin' radio down, or I'm comin' in there, and after I bust it up, I'll cut you."

From the other side of the door, Jackson responded, "Miz Macintosh, I dunno what you talkin' 'bout. I don't have no radio on. I was jes' settin' in here, watchin' fishin' on my television. I don't have no radio on."

"Jackson, don't you try to run no game on me, you li'l black motherfucker. I know what you're up to, tryin' to make me think I'm crazy. Well, I'm not so crazy I don't know when somebody's tryin' to make me think I'm crazy, and I'M NOT CRAZY, YOU HEAR ME! I AIN'T CRAZY."

Mrs. Washington, a downstairs neighbor, hearing all the unaccustomed noise, came out into the hall and looked up the stairs. She knew perfectly well that Anna Lee was absolutely and irrefutably crazy. Mrs. Washington was an LPN who had spent many a night on the ward at the nearby Homer G. Phillips Hospital and she knew schizophrenic hallucination when she saw it. She had been watching Anna Lee's deterioration for some time, undecided as to how or even if she should interfere. Well, decision time had arrived, although God knows, it was that same crazy dilemma which always faced her people: to turn in one of her own in order to protect one of her own, or just keep the white man out of their affairs. Finally, hearing the fear in poor Mr. Jackson's voice, between Anna Lee's threats and kicks, she called the police. After all the legal requirements were met, Anna Lee was carried off to the state hospital on Arsenal Street; it was over.

At the state hospital she was medicated enough to calm down and even play the out-of-tune piano in the day room. It was finally decided by the powers-that-be that she was no longer a threat to herself or anyone else and she was allowed to roam freely through the grounds. The medication that calmed her down, however, interfered significantly with her ability to think, or actually, to follow one train of thought through to the end. On top of that, in the early sixties the mental healing arts were focused almost exclusively on nurture, not nature. Anna Lee felt that if she heard one more question about penis envy or potty training she was going to have to find a way to kill herself. So one day, full of her own pain and loneliness, she simply wandered out the gate, never even looking back. Funding and staffing being what they are in state institutions, the attempt to locate and bring her back was half-hearted, and Anna Lee slipped through the large and well-known cracks of the system.

By the time she made her escape, Anna Lee had been in the state hospital for about six months, at which time she simply walked down the curving driveway to the sidewalk. She didn't even look back, knowing that they didn't have the personnel or the will to monitor everybody all the time. She still had some hope of putting her life back together as it had been. Maybe she could just go on, maybe let the doctors treat her and fill her with pills or whatever, and everything could just be the same again. She made her way to the Near North Side on Delmar, where her apartment was and stood across the street from it, looking up. She was dismayed to see that the curtains in her apartment were different; she saw the silhouette of a man through them. Who could be in her apartment? Who had changed the front room curtains? Then the curtains parted and a woman's smiling face looked out. It was a beautiful young and happy face that belonged to a black woman with close cropped hair. She looked like an African carving. A tall black man came out the front door of the building, looked up at the window, smiled and waved. Then he went to a Chevrolet on the street, got in, started up and drove away. With a sudden mental jerk, Anna Lee realized that somebody lived there in her apartment; that, in fact, it was no longer her apartment at all. It was home to someone else.

Well, then, what had become of her things, her belongings, her clothes, her lovely spinet piano? Her whole life had been up there in those five rooms. Where was her music, where were her books, her towels, her dishes, things she had treasured? Some of them had been heirlooms from her grandmother; the old pie safe, so old that it was held together not by nails and glue, but through doweling and careful dovetailing by some master carpenter.

She ran across the street and pounded on the downstairs door on the left. This was the apartment of Mrs. Washington, the woman who had called the police on Anna Lee on that fateful day. Anna Lee had no idea who had called them; in truth, the question had never occurred to her. Now she beat on Mrs. Washington's door in a frenzy of anxiety. She must know what happened; she must get her life back.

Mrs. Washington had always felt simply awful about that phone call she had made, even while acknowledging that it was the only thing to do. She had called the state hospital, but could get no information from the bureaucratic system and had finally given up. Also, she had to admit, even had she known, there was nothing she could do about it. The phone calls were merely a sop to her guilt, and that was something she was just going to have to live with, no matter how illogical it was.

On this day, she opened her door a crack and seeing Anna Lee's desperate face, almost jumped out of her skin. Then, that selfsame guilt seeing an opportunity to redeem itself, made her open the door wider and say, "Anna Lee! What in the world are you doing here, child?"

"Please, Mrs. Washington. Who's in my apartment? What happened to all my things, my piano? Please, I have to know, I have to know."

A terrible pity welled up in Mrs. Washington, and, without considering the danger she had perceived six months previously, she held the door open for Anna Lee and said gently, "Come on in, baby. Come on in, and I'll fix some nice hot tea."

As Mrs. Washington went back to the kitchen to prepare tea, Anna Lee stood in her living room. Although the contents of the rooms were different from her apartment upstairs, the layout of them was achingly familiar. She knew that the short hall that started out of the dining room led past a bathroom and into a kitchen. On the right of the hall, across from the bathroom, was the larger bedroom, and off the kitchen to the right was the smaller one. Going straight out the back kitchen door led to a small screened in porch with a short flight of steps into the back yard. Following the concrete walk to the back would lead either to an old garage or, where it veered to the left, a gate in the chain-link fence that surrounded the small yard. The gate opened into the alley where the two dumpsters were situated. Here, with all its beautiful familiarity, here was home, safety, where Anna Lee needed to be, where she **belonged**. She had to get back here, she had to get her things back, she had to, she must.

Mrs. Washington was coming through the hall carrying a tray with tea things on it. When she got into the dining room, she smiled reassuringly at Anna Lee even as she carefully navigated her way between the dining room table chairs on her right and the sideboard on her left, watchful lest she bump an elbow and have an accident. Passing through the archway that led into the living room she set the tray on the coffee table, sat down on the sofa, and with a pat of her hand on the sofa cushion next to her, invited Anna Lee to do the same.

Anna Lee sat down as bidden and looked at the tea things. They were set on a medium-sized tin tray, not a particularly expensive item, but pleasing to the eye, with a greeting-card picture of birds and flowers. On it was a tea set that consisted of a small white porcelain teapot, two matching cups with saucers, a creamer and sugar bowl. Mrs. Washington had also placed two spoons, a small stack of paper napkins and a plate of chocolate chip cookies on the tray. As she stared at it, Anna Lee realized that it had been at least six months since she had had any tea and cookies. All the little niceties, the amenities that make life fun, had disappeared. She had become a number in a large institution where she took meals with people with whom it was mostly impossible to have conversation; she slept in a dormitory situation where she had a locker which she could not lock, so that anything that she might have had that she wanted to keep was always in danger from one of the other patients. She had no privacy, no boundaries, and tea and chocolate chip cookies were just not a part of her life anymore. She did have access to a badly maintained piano in the day room, but the last time she had sat down to it one of the more manic patients went into a screeching fit that the piano was sending out signals to Venus that strengthened the death rays that were being directed at him from there. So, until his medication took effect (an iffy proposition at best), she couldn't ease her pain with what she loved most, pitiful facsimile though it was. Anna

Lee was disappearing, and it seemed that nothing could stop that unless she managed to get her life back. That's why she was here today.

Mrs. Washington poured out two cups of tea, and holding the saucer, handed one to Anna Lee. "So tell me, child, what are you doing here? Did you get some kind of furlough from the hospital?"

Anna Lee doctored her tea with cream and sugar, stirred it, set the cup down and rested the spoon on the saucer. All the while not looking at Mrs. Washington, trying to buy some time for herself, how she could explain that she had simply left on her own, nobody's permission, no overnight passes, just Anna Lee struggling to deal with a situation so alien to her. Finally she looked up at Mrs. Washington and said simply, "I left."

Mrs. Washington started and said, "But, baby, you need your medication. How can you get it out here? You could get hurt." She was also thinking that somebody else could get hurt, too, but she just didn't have it in her heart to make another phone call on Anna Lee. She just wasn't going to do it, no matter what the law said, or anybody else. She had been called on, done her duty on that terrible day, and now enough was enough. "Where you gonna live? What you gonna do?"

"Well, I was hoping I could get my old job back, get back into my apartment…." The rest remained unstated, and she dropped her eyes helplessly, looking at her hands limp in her lap. Then she looked up and said, "What became of my things, Mrs. Washington? Who has my piano?"

Mrs. Washington set her cup and saucer on the coffee table and looked at Anna Lee. Gently, she put her hand over Anna Lee's hands and said, "Baby, all your belongings were auctioned off. You know, you had a lease, and the real estate company had to make up the unpaid months. They brought in an auctioneer, and everything was sold, and then they re-let the apartment."

Anna Lee looked up, tears running down her face, and nodded dumbly. Mrs. Washington wanted nothing more fervently at that moment than to be someplace else, someplace very far away. Her heart ached for this lovely young talented woman. Her future had been so very bright such a short time ago.

Anna Lee stood up and said, "Thank you for the tea and your time, Mrs. Washington. You were always a good friend and neighbor to me. Give my regards to Mr. Washington," and started for the door. Every syllable was a knife thrust into Mrs. Washington's heart.

Back out on the street Anna Lee made her

way south and east to the intersection of Olive and Boyle Avenues. It took awhile because she was on foot, but one thing she had these days was time, so that didn't matter. This was the locale of Gaslight Square, and this was where the night spot/restaurant called Nick the Greek's Restaurant & Bistro sat in Victorian splendor. Anna Lee had put in several years there as the featured entertainment and she thought that if she talked to Horace, if he could see that she was okay again, he might give her back her old job. This was her last hope; without it she might as well be dead.

By the time she got there, the sun was going down. It was a beautiful May evening, the air was light and delicious-smelling; couples were strolling along, going from bistro to bistro. All the restaurants here were four stars; any one of them could provide a gourmet meal. The bars specialized in the best entertainment to be found in St. Louis; good musicians and good singers of every genre could be heard here. Anna Lee stood in the middle of the sidewalk across the street from Nick the Greek's while foot traffic flowed around her. Laughing people, happy people out to have a fun evening. Nobody drove in Gaslight Square, it was all on foot and on a beautiful night like this everyone was feeling friendly.

Anna Lee gathered herself together and

went to the door of Nick the Greek's Restaurant & Bistro. She knew she looked disreputable, but what was she going to do? All of her clothes had apparently been auctioned off with everything else, and she had had to sort through the rummage closet they kept at the hospital. Charitable donations frequently were limited to clothing, and the items were kept for the indigent patients. Anna Lee's choices, due to her heroic height, were even more limited. So in her baggy maroon corduroy pants and stained sweatshirt she decided to take her chances with Horace.

When she got to the door she patted her hair unconsciously, a gesture that she had always had when she felt a little unsure. A new face at the door, a small man in a tuxedo, looked at her with distaste and told her to go around to the kitchen door if she wanted a handout. Apparently the generous policy with street people hadn't changed, just the gatekeeper. Anna Lee looked at him and said, "I'd like to see Horace, if you please."

"Mr. Kapandopoulos is busy. As I said, if you need something to eat, please go to the kitchen door, but please do not continue to stand there in the doorway. We have customers coming in."

Just then, one of the waiters, an older black man dressed in black trousers, starched white shirt and black bow tie, was passing carrying a tray full of dirty dishes. He looked at Anna Lee, said, "Pardon me," and then stopped and turned around. "Anna Lee, is that you?"

Anna Lee smiled radiantly. Here, at last, was someone from her past who was glad to see her, who had retained a memory of who she really was, not this wretched woman in ill-fitting mismatched clothes. "Hi, Charles, how're you doin'? Grandbabies doin' alright?"

Charles set the tray down and took one of her hands in both of his calloused ones. "Anna Lee, you are surely a sight for sore eyes." Just then the little man in the tuxedo, a maitre d' who clearly enjoyed his authority, gave Charles a hard stare. "Why don't you go 'round back to the kitchen and I'll catch up with you there. There's those back there who would love to see you." With a wink, he said, "Gotta take care of my customers. Else how'm I gonna make my tips?"

Just as Charles started to pick up his tray Horace Kapandopoulos came out of the hall that led to his office and noticed the little knot of three people up front. As a good host it was his business to see that everything ran smoothly, and this looked a little odd, the tall black woman dressed in strange clothes and his maitre d' with a seriously pained look on his face. "Arthur, is everything all right here?" He looked at the woman, and then again, and took in a quick short breath. Repeating the wonder that Charles had just uttered, he said, "Anna Lee, is that you?"

Again, so grateful to have her identity reaffirmed, she nodded with a great huge grin. "Yes, Horace, it's me, and I've come to see you."

"My dear, what a pleasure; what an unmitigated pleasure." He looked around and said, "Come on with me back to the office. We'll get you something to eat and have a talk." Then, to poor Arthur's chagrin the boss walked this derelict woman right through the dining room full of customers and on to the back.

Horace unlocked his office door, held it open for Anna Lee to precede him. When he got in he gestured to a chair and sat down behind his desk, which was clearly chosen for service and convenience, not looks.

In fact everything about the office screamed efficiency, which was something Horace Kapandopoulos understood. He had come up in the restaurant business started by his father, Nicholas Kapandopoulos. Nicholas had arrived in the U.S. in the first decade of the twentieth century, not much more than a lad himself. Eventually, he and his new bride managed to open a small restaurant in New York City that did all right. But Prohibition came, and with it, the necessity to turn a nice little restaurant into a speakeasy. Then the rivalries among the bootleggers began to take their toll among the business owners, each gang demanding that the owners purchase exclusively from them with the threat of dire consequences if the owners did not comply. As the competition among the gangs grew, one night after closing the Kapandopoulos restaurant exploded, as a warning to Nick. Nick had a young son by then, little Horace, and a baby girl. He and Kiki simply liquidated everything they could, packed up the boy and their baby girl and moved to St. Louis in the hope that they could escape the worst of the violence. There Nick and Kiki joined the St. Nicholas Greek Orthodox Church which occupied a sizeable piece of real estate on the corner of Forest Park Boulevard and Kingshighway. Nick felt that since the church was named for his patron saint it was a good omen. So they opened another small restaurant which sold no sub-rosa liquor. It was located on Euclid Avenue close to the church, and the Kapandopouloses lived in the apartment above it. The restaurant and family both prospered; Horace worked in the family business after school, mopping floors, keeping the kitchen and restrooms spotlessly clean; he bused tables, ran the cash register, and became a superb maker of the wonderful cuisine of Asia Minor. Finally the business grew to a point where larger quarters were required. Nick and Kiki bought a home on Maryland Place and the restaurant was moved to Gaslight Square, just as that area was beginning to come into its own.

Now, at age 45, Horace Kapandopoulos had become a savvy restauranteur, having taken the reins from his father's hands. Nick still stepped in from time to time, but mostly he trusted his son's judgment which had repeatedly shown itself to be excellent. Horace, as his father before him, treated his employees like family. His wife, Elena, did a lot of the administrative work, such as bookkeeping and payroll, in between raising her own three children, but they always had time for their people. It was understood that happy employees made for good business, and turnover in this restaurant was rare.

Horace picked up his phone and punched the button marked "kitchen" while holding up the index finger from his other hand to indicate to Anna Lee to have patience, he would be with her in a minute. The kitchen answered and Horace said, "Paulie, I've got Anna Lee in my office right now…Yes, yes, I know. Of course I'll send her back, that's why I'm calling you. Fix her whatever she wants, see that she's well fed. Yeah, I'll let you know," and hung up.

Now, as he sat there behind his desk

looking at Anna Lee, his undiluted pleasure at seeing her came into conflict with the concern that he was beginning to feel as he got a really good look at her. "How are you, Anna Lee, I mean, how are you, really? Tell me how I can help."

"Horace, I know I look like fido right now, and I probably have some nerve. But I need work, I need my job back." She looked at him imploringly. "Horace, don't you see, I've got to get things together again."

Affection and discomfort went to war on Horace's face. Gently he said, "Anna Lee, when we first heard what happened to you, we tried to find you. It was useless. Elena spent more than several days on the phone trying to get through the red tape. Because we weren't strictly speaking family, we just got the run-around. People would say they couldn't find your file, and would we call back. We'd call back and get somebody else who would take a message and promise a call back, or that somebody would be in touch with us, but it never happened." He sighed. "Those people can just wear you down. Finally, we understood: we were not going to get anything from those people. In the meantime, I still had a business to run; people would come in looking for you, and when you weren't here, they'd just leave. I had to hire somebody to replace you. He doesn't sing as well as you, but he's a very good entertainer, he interacts with the audience, clowns a little bit, and folks seem to like him. I can't just let him go, Anna Lee. That wouldn't be right." He shifted in his chair. "But I'll tell you what I CAN do: I'll be happy to put you to work in the kitchen, they always need help back there, and in time, who knows what will work out. You got a place to stay?"

Softly, Anna Lee answered, "No."

"Well, be here at closing time. Elena will be overjoyed to put you up. We've been so worried about you and didn't know what to do. You come on back to the house with me, and in the morning, we'll see what we can work out, okay?"

She nodded and said, "Okay," but of course she didn't show up that night or ever again. She knew she needed employment so that she could stay off the streets and out of jail. But there was more than one reason she didn't want the Kapandopouloses' help. First of all, she knew that she had done something pretty bad to get herself locked up in the first place, some vague memory of threatening someone with a knife; so she knew that it was not at all unlikely that the law wanted her. What had she been thinking of, coming to Horace anyway? She couldn't involve him and Elena in something like that. In Missouri, a run-in with the law could cost Horace his liquor license. Secondly (and this was a powerful reason), her heart shrank from watching somebody else do what she so loved to do. It wasn't false pride; she didn't think she was too good to work in the kitchen. It was the feeling that something that she loved had been arbitrarily taken from her and given to someone else. It was like having a beloved bicycle taken and being forced to watch the thief enjoy it, while being powerless to get it back. There was this feeling that she had been shut out from everything she loved by a glass wall and she had no idea why, but she was now barred from everything that was dear to her, even though she could watch as everybody but her had access. Like Milton's Satan, she had been consigned to outer darkness, but had no idea why. Why was she being punished? What had she done to merit this treatment? For the rest of her life, all she would be able to do would be to watch through the glass while everybody else lived their lives, and she had none.

That night she found a dumpster in a secluded courtyard of an apartment building and managed to get in between it and the brick wall of the garage. She slept there pretty uncomfortably, but no one would have guessed she was there, and that was what she wanted more than comfort. She was awakened by the sound of the city trash truck trundling down the alley. She knew that the dumpster she was hiding behind was about to be picked up and moved by two able-bodied young men, and its contents dumped into the truck. She had to move if she didn't want to be seen and possibly arrested for vagrancy.

She moved out of the alley onto the street, where she made her way over to Newstead Avenue. This was a neighborhood that was rapidly becoming blighted. When she was a child it hadn't been quite so bad, but everybody knew it was going. For one thing, the phenomenon that would become known as white flight was happening, all the middle class white families fled in terror as "those coloreds" moved in. And when they went, they took with them the grocery stores and small businesses, the beauty parlors, the drugstores, the insurance agencies, the dentists and doctors that had thrived there so long. What was left were small liquor stores that sold sweets, lunch meat and bread, some milk and related items at outrageous prices because they had a captive audience. White landlords who lived in the suburbs rented out the buildings and their apartments without a thought to who was occupying them, just as long as they could collect the rent, which was unjustifiably high.

None of that money ever went into upkeep of the buildings, for which these landlords took a huge tax write-off, and their occupants became the landlords' prisoners, unable to scrape enough money together to get away. Some of the buildings were now vacant, windows boarded, and became a breeding ground for various types of vermin and crime; juvenile gangs met here, they were a good place for rapists to operate, and the heroin addicts could access their private heaven in the dark, smelly corners.

She passed weed-grown vacant lots, where buildings had once stood, but fire (always a hazard in empty buildings) and just general neglect had taken them down. The lots had become dumps full of broken half-pint liquor and pop bottles, soda cans, cellophane cigarette packs, even in some of them broken furniture. The word, "eyesore," had found a home.

Moving north on Newstead she knew would take her to her childhood home. She didn't know what she expected to find there, but she had felt safe there as a child, so like a homing pigeon that's where she headed. Maybe on the way, she might find something to eat. Sure enough, just a couple of blocks up she found a Salvation Army outreach storefront where she could get fed, if she'd only sit still for the sermon. She got into line and pretty soon found herself sitting in a folding chair in a small makeshift chapel along with other derelicts, many of whom smelled very badly. "I guess hygiene isn't that big a deal when you're hungry," thought Anna Lee. Some of the eyes she looked into were blank, others dropped, while yet others stared back belligerently.

All of this faded into the background when the young woman in the blue uniform came up the podium and said, "Let's praise the Lord in song. Please open the books you found to hymn number 79." It was *How Great Thou Art*, a song Anna Lee remembered from her days with her grandmother at the Baptist church. She looked at the music and tears came to her eyes. Just to be looking at sheet music again, oh, what a joy! She opened her mouth and the song came pouring out of her heart. Her voice was a little rusty from disuse, but the key was comfortable and Anna Lee soon found her voice which soared over the half-hearted attempts of her fellow worshippers; some of them looked at her surreptitiously and then fell into the music with some gusto, encouraged by her vigorous singing. Her appreciation reached greater heights as she listened to the piano. This was an upright, a well cared-for instrument, and it filled Anna Lee with delight and a real determination to get her hands onto it. Nor was this lost on the young woman leading the group and she made a mental note to speak with this tall young black woman after services. This young lady had some real promise and the young soldier for the Lord saw some opportunity here.

Except for the intervals involving singing, Anna Lee was restless and inattentive during the services. All she could think about was that piano and when the last "amen" was finally uttered, while the others jumped and ran for the door into the dining room, Anna Lee, her hunger forgotten, made her way through the chairs to the corner where it sat. Her progress was intercepted by the young woman in uniform. "Hi, I'm Lt. Shirley Wilbourne," she said, holding out her hand. "But everybody just calls me Shirley or Shirl," she smiled. "I noticed during services that you seem to have some real feeling for the Lord, and you certainly have the voice to express it."

Anna Lee was embarrassed to say that feeling for the Lord had nothing to do with it, it was music; music owned her, body and soul and except for the occasional playing at the hospital, she had been too long deprived of it. She took the offered hand and said, "Thank you. I was wondering if......," here she was a little stymied, and didn't know quite how to put it. "Would it cause a problem if I played the piano for a while?" She didn't want to explain her circumstances, how badly she missed playing, so she just said, "That's a really nice piano, really good tone. Would anybody mind?"

Lt. Wilbourne smiled and said, "I don't think anybody'd mind. Just don't be too late getting your breakfast, because there's only a limited amount out there, and some of these folks have been hungry a long time. But go ahead, enjoy yourself," and she turned to the door.

Anna Lee didn't even take the time to watch Shirley leave. She sat down on the bench, adjusted herself and then went into Ellington's *Solitude.* Shirley stopped at the doorway when she heard the chords. "Oh, boy, I think I might've have scored big time here. Thank you, Lord," she breathed, and then went on out to find her supervisor and tell her about Anna Lee.

As she segued from tune to tune, sometimes singing with them, sometimes not, Anna Lee completely forgot the time and the demands of her stomach. She was in the middle of a medley from Gershwin's *Catfish Row* when a soft "hello" broke into her reverie. She stopped playing and looked up at an older woman. The woman, like young Shirley, was wearing a dark blue uniform, only hers had an impressive array of decorations. She was holding a tray on which sat what looked to Anna Lee like an egg-and-bacon sandwich, a half-pint carton of milk, an orange and a cup of coffee. The woman set the tray on top of the piano and sat down next to Anna Lee. "I was afraid you were not going to get your breakfast, so I brought it to you. Please eat and then continue playing if you wish." She smiled. "The only proviso is that I get to listen."

Anna Lee was much moved by the kindness they were showing her here. She introduced herself and thanked the woman profusely, who simply smiled and nodded. Then she picked up the sandwich and almost inhaled it. She had forgotten how hungry she was and now, she was feeling so much better.

As she peeled the orange the woman said, "I'm General Bernice Allison. Lt. Wilbourne told me you were here playing, but I thought she had to be exaggerating about your skill. Now I know she wasn't. You must have been playing most of your life, is that right? I mean, you are still a young woman, but your dexterity is quite remarkable. Also, I'm impressed with your knowledge of harmonics. How are you with classical?"

Anna Lee paused as she thought. "Yes, of course, I had to start with the classics." She chuckled. "Yes, in fact my first cross-over piece was a small Bach thing." Then she laughed openly. "I was so proud when I mastered that. I was seven years old."

Bernice said, "Do you mind?" and proceeded to play a short passage from a Bach fugue. "There now, recognize it?"

Anna Lee smiled and said, "Of course, that's the Little Organ Fugue, the one in D major. One of my favorites, as a matter of fact," and she went on to add several bars to what Bernice had played. Then, with Bernice doing the treble and Anna Lee playing bass, they finished it out, all four hands flying in perfect synchronization. When it was over they laughed and hugged, and Anna Lee was brought back with a start to her sad reality. How long had it been since she'd been hugged? How long since anyone had touched her except to restrain her? She began to tear up and grabbed one of the paper napkins from the tray Bernice had brought in.

Bernice cupped Anna Lee's chin and lifted her head. "Anna Lee, we can help you here. Whatever your story is, whatever demons pursue you, we can help you. God can handle anything you put at his feet. How about it? We can put you to work here at the mission, you can start in the kitchen, but you'll play at all our services. In fact, I promise you free access to the piano except when it is needed for worship. We need you here, God needs you here. He gave you a wonderful gift. How about giving some of it back to Him?"

Such conflict arose in Anna Lee's breast! Serve God? Wasn't He the one responsible for the pickle she was in right now? On the other hand, it was so tempting to say yes to the perks that included the piano. How wonderful that would be. But Anna Lee was afraid, afraid she'd be found out. She was ashamed of what those people at the hospital had called her paranoid schizophrenia. She didn't want these lovely people to know. The first time she had ever heard those words she was a child listening to the radio with her grandmother. They were listening to a program called *The Shadow* which her grandmother adored. Bad guys bit the dust when The Shadow caught up with them. But she had heard the lead character, Lamont Cranston, describe a criminal as a "paranoid schizophrenic." When she asked her grandmother what that meant, her grandmother had patted her hand and said, "A disease of the mind, baby, a disease of the mind. Makes you do bad things, whether you want to or not. Just thank the Lord above that we don't have none o' that." And now, here she was, carrying the shameful label herself. As she heard it in the movies and saw it in the books she read she began to understand that society regarded people like her as a public menace and felt that for their protection, both hers and theirs, she needed to be in custodial care. She couldn't tell this kind, soft-spoken woman that she had these fits over which she had no control, fits in which she heard loud, discordant music in her head. In the last month in the hospital, right before she was due for her next dose of medication, a new wrinkle had been added to the music: voices that said horrible things to her, told her to do horrible things. She would cover her ears, and still she heard them. This didn't happen all the time, but she was in such dread of the voices that once or twice she thought about doing what they told her to do. Maybe that would shut them up. How could she explain to this woman sitting next to her that she had days in which she was lost to the rational world; could she make her understand that these spells were only temporary? Surely this information would frighten her. But if she could tell her, and perhaps they could arrange to get medication for her, maybe this might yet work out. Maybe there was hope. But how to do it was the problem. She had to think on it some. "Thank you, General, for your offer. I'd like to give it some thought, if I may. There are things that I have to figure out." Yeah, like how to explain that she was a fugitive from the state mental facility. Ooh, boy, there was a problem.

The general just smiled a gentle smile and

said, "Take your time, Anna Lee. I know this must mean a major life change for you. But I think you have had some experience with major life changes now, haven't you. Give it some thought and we'll talk tonight after dinner, or better yet, tomorrow morning. Maybe sleeping on it will help. You can eat here, and we have some beds that we sometimes use when the Emergency Lodge has an overflow. You can put up there, and we'll talk after breakfast." Ah, a little light. Maybe there was a caring God after all.

Anna spent the better part of the day walking around her old neighborhood. She was feeling fairly buoyant because she was beginning to feel some hope about her situation. Maybe that nice white woman really could help her, get her off the street and keep the hospital people away from her. Maybe she really could use the piano again, play and sing to her heart's content. If she could, oh, boy, if she could she would show God her gratitude.

Thinking these thoughts, she stopped in front of a little concrete block building. It stood where the Baptist church had once been that she had attended with her grandmother. Now, instead of the frame building with the steeple, there was this little obscenity, with barred windows and blinking neon signs that advertised liquor and cigarettes. Anna Lee wondered what they sold out the back door. The building was surrounded by a black tar parking lot littered with gum, candy and cigarette wrappers with complete disregard for the trash can standing close to the door. Oh, thank You, Lord, that Nanna couldn't see this. If she wasn't already dead these three years, this would kill her. It just seemed to Anna Lee that everything she held dear was evaporating in front of her eyes. But the woman, Bernice Allison, had offered her something else, a replacement. Maybe it wasn't what she was used to, the status and prestige she had had in the musical community before, the privacy and comfort of her own apartment, but it was a beginning, and Anna Lee was sure that it could only get better. And to be sure, at this point the only way she could go had to be up. So she felt good and she felt hopeful, believing that there might be release from this whatever-it-was she found herself in.

  She returned to the mission later that afternoon, and she was put to work in the kitchen, her long fingers flying as she peeled potatoes. She played and sang at evening services, and after dinner she helped clean up. By the time she was shown to her bed in the small four-bed dormitory, she was sure that in the morning she could give a grateful and unequivocal "yes" to General Allison's invitation.

Anna Lee woke up just before dawn, the discordant music clanging in her head, not sure exactly where she was. All she could think of was shutting it down; that was her first priority. She looked around her and remembered where she was. Maybe if she got out of here she could find some relief. She was away from the hospital now and had no way of obtaining the medication that temporarily stopped the racket. She thought about Bernice Allison and realized that there was no way she could tell her what was going on inside her head. It was just too shameful; she might frighten the general. No, she had to get out of here. This God that everyone talked about had failed her once again; her last hope was shattered. She sat there a minute on the narrow bed, hands twisted into fists. She squeezed them so hard that her nails dug into her palms and drew blood. Why, why, why? What had she done to deserve this? Quietly sobbing, she wiped her palms on her sweatshirt sleeves, then made up the bed. After that she pulled off the nightdress that had been given to her by the mission which she folded up and lovingly laid on the pillow, the embodiment of the hope she had thought was hers. She pulled on her underwear and then the corduroy pants, and finally the sweatshirt streaked with her blood. She slipped her feet into the cheap loafers she had been given at the hospital and tiptoed out of the room. There was nobody else in it, but she didn't know who was up and around in the building and she didn't want to see anybody, or, more accurately, she didn't want anybody to see her. She crept down the stairs, a silent shadow in the early dawn, out the back door and onto the street, where she would remain for the next thirty-seven years.

Because she was still beautiful, she realized some fair success panhandling. Because she was big, the sexual predators steered clear of her. In the meantime, the terrible racket in her head continued intermittently, until she discovered that, for a dollar, she could buy a bottle of Ripple, which, while it didn't turn it off, made it tolerable. She had some good days; her torment seemed to be cyclical, and, while she never bothered to chart it, she began to recognize its onset, much as an epileptic could recognize an imminent seizure. The everyday sounds around her became distant, had an echo, and soon the noise would begin.

As she became a familiar sight on the Row, the waters of the homeless subculture parted to admit her, and she found a place in that society of the nameless. She was quiet most of the time, minded her own business. Mostly, she was simply stunned, and still trying to process this monumental and abrupt change in her life. Like most people, she searched in her mind for a cause-and-effect relationship between her behavior and her current circumstances. She needed desperately to be able to explain it to herself. Slowly, as she ruminated on all the newness, bonds were formed; down here, there are no ethnic differences. Everyone is in the same disabled boat, just waiting for the final swamping.

Soon the weaker ones discovered that Anna Lee was a good friend when the bullies were on a rampage. That's how she acquired poor old Willie the Wino. Willie the Wino was a wet-brain, and the only idea left in it was his next drink. But some atavistic drive told him that if he wanted to survive to get that next drink, he should stick with Anna Lee. Anna Lee had intervened when another severely impaired drunk had tried forcibly to deprive Willie of a bottle he had managed to steal. Anna Lee had appeared in the alley just as the offender was trying to run off, Willie fiercely clinging to his tattered coattail. Anna Lee was beginning to swell with bloat from drinking and poor nutrition and as she bore down the alley she must have looked like the Angel of Death, black and huge, materializing out of nowhere.

She slammed the would-be bottle-snatcher against the wall, and, getting up close into his face, said, "Gimme that bottle." Paralyzed with fear and surprise, Anna Lee had no trouble prying the offender's fingers off the neck. She handed it to Willie without ever taking her eyes off the thief's face.

"Now, asshole, you apologize to Willie."

Apology hastily stammered, flight accomplished, and Willie knew he had found a friend. Thereafter, she was never out of his sight. Anna Lee stoically accepted his drunken gratitude-cum-adoration. She was frequently impatient with his incoherence, but his tenacious presence was a comfort to her; protecting him gave some kind of purpose to what was now an aimless life.

What eventually became clear to observers was that, because of Anna Lee's chemical pathology, what was a normal adrenaline rush for someone else became a flood of aggression in her when aroused. This, combined with her height and ever-increasing bulk, made her a formidable adversary.

Her reputation as Peacekeeper & Defender of the Weak was sealed the day she took on the Big Biker. Nobody ever knew where the Big Biker came from, but that was not unusual down here. He didn't own a bike, either, but he dressed like a fugitive from Hell's Angels, and liked to flaunt his tattoos. One of them was a voluptuous naked woman on his left bicep; when he flexed the muscle, she undulated sensuously. He had an Oriental dragon on his fat, hairy belly, and when he was drunk, which was most of the time, he liked to pull up his leather vest and talk to it. He called it Archie, and he would say, "Archie, this fuckin' bottle dint last no time a-tall. What we gonna do, now, Archie, huh?" Sometimes he would curse the dragon, and blame it for his misfortune; sometimes he would stroke it and tell it all his plans of getting back on the road again, with a big hog between his thighs, and feel the wind in his hair.

One day, the Big Biker staggered into the alley and flopped down with his back to the wall. While he was engaged in a monologue with Archie, he happened to spot the little kitten that Anna Lee had rescued.

She had acquired it because somebody had put it into a bag, tied a string around it and dumped it into the sewer. She heard its little whimperings and mewlings and after a bit of stretching was able to reach what looked like a brown paper bag doing some kind of dance. She fed the little thing scraps and kept it with her at night, under her coat. She had immediately fallen in love with it, the way Lennie in *Of Mice and Men* loved soft, furry things. The sheer need for tactile contact with another warm body was sometimes overwhelming. Anna Lee, for all that she was on the Row, was fastidious, and the thought of stroking Willie and his ilk was inconceivable. This little creature was the recipient of all the pent up love in Anna Lee's passionate heart. Here was something, something that brought a little grace and beauty into her life; something she could love and loved her back.

She usually kept it in her large coat pocket, but this particular day had been one of her bad days, and she had forgotten her precious kitty. The clatter in her head drowned out all other sound, and she was intent on the business of obtaining a bottle to quiet it down. So the little kitty was forgotten and left to crouch down by the grate in the alley where they had spent the previous night, the little thing comforted by the smell of Anna Lee. The Big Biker had long coveted that place by the grate that was generally acknowledged as Anna Lee's exclusive preserve. Furthermore, he was damned sick and tired of this bitch, the way everybody danced to her fuckin' tune. In between remarks to Archie, he cocked a lustful eye in the direction of the desired site, and lo, there was the kitten. He reached over, grabbed its little neck, and held it up, looking at it.

It dangled and squealed, and one of the motionless lumps in the alley reared up and said, "Man, you wanna keep your stones, leave that li'l shit factory alone. That's Anna Lee's."

The Big Biker, his manhood offended by the suggestion that he should fear Anna Lee, shot back, "Shut the fuck up, dirtbag. I do what I want; and besides, she's just a bitch. I don't take shit from bitches."

With that he chuckled obscenely, pulled out an old pocketknife with half a handle and committed an act of unspeakable sadism on the little animal. He was a man of action, not just one of these fuckin' dirtbags who laid here in the alley and talked about all the shit they was gonna do and all the ass they was gonna kick.

Several of the alley's denizens who were still conscious looked with horror, both at the act itself and the violence it presaged. Anna Lee was not going to like this.

A couple of days later, when Anna Lee was finally back to semi-normal, she woke up hungry. The first thing she did was look for her kitten, gingerly patting down Willie's unconscious back as he lay there snoring. Well, it had wandered off, but it'd be back. In the meantime, the best thing would be to hunt up some food for herself and her baby. She wandered off to look in a dumpster behind a coffee shop in the neighborhood, and found there the mutilated body of the kitten where some well-meaning soul, in an attempt to avoid mayhem, had thought to hide it from Anna Lee. Her wordless horror was soon replaced by a rage that drove, propelled, **demanded** some kind of action. She went back to her place in the alley and kicked Willie until he came to. She grabbed his collar, and pulled his groggy face close to her, oblivious to the sour smell that was a combination of filth, cheap booze, vomit and urine.

"Who killed my kitty," she demanded without preamble.

"Geez, Anna Lee, what the fuck," and he twisted, trying to extricate himself from her grasp and go back to lala-land.

She slapped his face and said again, "Who killed my kitty?"

At that point, a skinny drunk who always wore an old slouch hat, looked up blearily and said to Anna Lee, "That fat fucker who wears leather."

"Thanks, Slim, thank you very much," she said softly, and went on the hunt.

She found the Big Biker out back by the dumpster behind Father Leon's mission, talking to Archie, and holding court among the other drunks and addicts who liked to lounge around that area. She came up behind him quietly and swiftly, and grabbed his long, greasy hair, jerking him down backwards onto his knees. Before he could recover from his surprise, she pushed him all the way down onto his back, and flopped on top of him, straddling his belly. As he reached up to push her off, she grabbed his right arm and started working on the fingers of that hand. The pain was excruciating and all he could think of was separating this demon from his hand. During the entire performance, Anna Lee had not uttered a sound, except for the occasional grunt of effort. Her face was rigid, her eyes crazed, and as the Big Biker looked up at her, he knew he was outclassed.

One of the onlookers began screeching with fear, and Father Leon came out back to see what the racket was about. Father Leon was a tall, slim black man, born and raised in the Republic of Cameroon. His speech was still scattershot with the strongly articulated consonants of his native tongue.

"Anna Lee," laying his hand on her shoulder, "Anna Lee, come now, get off him."

Anna Lee appeared to hear nothing except the popping of the Big Biker's metacarpals under her relentless pressure. Each snap elicited a widening of Anna Lee's grinning mouth. The screams from the Big Biker were music to her enraged ears, drowning out the frightened witnesses.

"Anna Lee," raising his voice, Father Leon put his hand under her chin and redirected her gaze, "Anna Lee, you must stop. Now!"

At this point, plainclothes detective, Lt. Frank O'Meara of St. Louis' finest, came out, slightly breathless, hand in his sports jacket, ready to pull his weapon. With a fast, controlled chop onto Anna Lee's shoulder, he broke her grip. She looked up at him, stunned, the glaze of rage beginning to fade from her eyes.

"He killed my kitty, Mr. O'Meara, he did things to that kitty……. He killed my baby." She began to sob. "That li'l kitty didn't hurt anybody, Mr. O'Meara, she didn't hurt anybody." She wiped her nose on her sleeve, and covered her face with her hands.

Father Leon put his arm around her and led her through the door into the kitchen of the mission. There, at a rickety table covered with a red-and-white checked oilcloth that had seen better days in an Italian restaurant, he sat her down and said, "Here, Anna Lee," and gave her a cup of coffee from the big stainless steel urn that was always going. She accepted the coffee, again wiping her nose with her sleeve, and just stared wordlessly into the cup. Father Leon silently handed her his handkerchief and waited, knowing that Anna Lee was sparing of words.

Lt. O'Meara stuck his head into the open door and said, "Lee, I gotta go and save you people from the bad guys. Catch you later."

"Yeah, Frank, just remember, I have your king in check."

"Yeah, right. When I come back, I'm bringin' a Polaroid. I'm tired of you cheatin' while I'm out fightin' crime."

Leon laughed and said, "Frank, it would be a complete waste of time for you to take pictures because you are beyond help."

Their chess game had been running for something like fifteen years, nobody had won yet and there were those who suspected that great pains were taken on either side to insure that this would never happen.

Anna Lee looked up over her coffee cup, and set it on the table. "Father," she began slowly, "I'm sorry I caused such a ruckus in your yard. I don't mean to be mean to anybody. It's just that, well, sometimes I don't understand. I mean," she said, warming up to her thoughts, "I was raised up not to blaspheme, you know? It took me years to stop blaming God for," she looked down at herself, gesturing from her shoulders to her knees with both hands, "what's become of me. I don't understand why I'm here instead of where I started out, and bad as it hurts sometimes, I know I just have to live with it. At first, I prayed for deliverance, and when I saw I wasn't gonna get it, why, I just started askin' for help to get me through the day, one day at a time. I thought maybe the kitty was an answer to that prayer. I know this sounds silly comin' from me, but, Father, you gotta love somethin'. And I thought maybe God had sent that little animal to bless me. She didn't hurt anybody; all she did was be cute. She couldn't defend herself, and she didn't hurt anybody. Why'd He allow that shi.... 'scuse me, Father, why'd He let that pig to do her that way? It's bad enough he killed her, but the way he did it is hard to forgive."

    She stopped here, seeming to have run out of words, and took a sip of her coffee, tears slowly running down her cheeks. Leon, sitting across the table from her, leaned forward. "Anna Lee, I don't have easy answers to the questions you ask. Bless your heart, I know that you hurt and I'm so sorry. I'd give anything to be able to wipe it all out for you, anything." He reached across the table, took his rumpled handkerchief from her unresisting fingers, and tenderly wiped her face.

    She ponderously rose without a word and went looking for poor old Willie the Wino.

Willie's brain, though now reduced by alcohol to its most basic functions, could operate with a cunning and stealth that rivaled the big jungle cats, when necessary. Anna Lee got him to steal four pints of MD/20-20 and drank herself into a stupor.

Jason snuggled down into Anna Lee's arms, at first tentatively, and then with a will. He had been afraid that perhaps she smelled badly, living out there on the street. He didn't know that one of Anna Lee's major acts of defiance against her condition was attention to hygiene. Down here on the Row, (which wasn't actually a row at all, but a circuit), there were several places: Father Leon's mission, the Salvation Army lodge, Rev. Joe Reis's shelter, a Lighthouse of Salvation, and the Mission of Mercy. These were dotted around the perimeter of the territory claimed by Anna Lee and her peers, and she would use the wash-up facilities of each, dividing her visits so that she did not make herself unwelcome in any one place. The people who ran these establishments understood exactly what she was doing, and made sure that soap and paper towels were available to her. Anna Lee always felt better after a good wash, and sometimes, when she just couldn't stand him anymore, she made poor old Willie the Wino go wash up, too. So Jason settled down into Anna Lee's soft and generous bosom, and allowed himself to relax. Anna Lee began to gently rock and croon. She still had a rich, soothing contralto, and Jason felt its spell. As she held him and stroked him, all the pain of his young heart welled up; he buried his face in her and began to cry, silent, hot tears of rage and self-loathing. She felt them soaking through her sweater, and just held him closer, patting his hair and humming.

"We'll sort this all out in the mornin', baby. Don't you worry about anything, you hear? Anna Lee's here, an' you'll be just fine."

Chapter Two

DAY ONE, January 29th Dawn broke, bright and clear, on a cold day. A sharp wind chased loose newspapers, which skittered up the alley, and plastered themselves against walls. Another bitterly cold day, when homelessness was most acutely felt by its membership who could still think about it. Another day to be faced, to keep body and soul together, find that next drink, try to keep out of the wind, and all the time wonder (if you still could) why you were even bothering to do it.

Jason, clutched in Anna Lee's embrace, stirred as she tried to sit up, having forgotten that she had him in her arms. She felt the unaccustomed weight and looked down at his blonde head. Ah, yes, here was that beautiful white child with no name. Well, we'd find out all about it over breakfast.

But first, "Boy, wake up, boy." She gently shook him and stroked his head.

Jason's eyes opened and he looked up uncomprehendingly into Anna Lee's face. Then he, too, remembered the night before, and wariness replaced wonder.

"It's all right, boy," Anna Lee said. "We just have to get some things straight. First off, what's your name?"

"Jason."

"Well, Jason, you can call me Anna Lee, and here's how it is. I'm gonna go over to Father Leon's mission and get us some breakfast. Now, you can't go with me, 'cause the first thing, Father'll ask about you, who you are and all that, and the next thing you know, there'll be uniforms and social workers all over the place, and you'll be in Juvie. You understand?"

"Yes, ma'm."

Anna Lee liked the "ma'm"; it wasn't often that she heard the amenities, and she appreciated it. Also, all her alarm bells were going off: she was savvy enough to know that something was very wrong here, and, beyond curiosity, she was interested in seeing the right thing done. Having had her own experience with the keepers of the world, she was cautious about turning Jason over to them.

"Now, you wait right here. I'll be a little while, because Father doesn't give doggie bags, I'll have to eat at his table. So I'll stay there and eat like always. So, and this is the important part, I'll have to steal some food to bring back to you, and Father, he's sharp. If he sees me hightailin' it out the door with a pocketful of food, he's gonna wanna know why. So I have to be real careful about swipin' stuff. OK?

"Now, you wait right here. Don't go

anywhere and don't talk to anybody, and I mean, nobody, you understand?"

Jason looked down at the sleeping Willie. Willie was snoring deeply and peacefully.

"Don't worry' 'bout Willie, boy," said Anna Lee, following his gaze. "He doesn't hurt anybody."

And she started off down the alley. When she got to the mouth, she stopped abruptly, and, turning around, came running back with surprising speed, considering her size. She grabbed Jason's arm and said, "I changed my mind. You're comin' with me."

She didn't stop to tell the startled Jason that she had remembered what had happened to her kitten and that she was taking no chances with him.

When they got to Father Leon's Mission, she took Jason around back, and told him to sit behind the rusty old dumpster and wait. Again, she told him to speak to no one, and she'd be back as soon as she could. She went inside, and Jason sat out there on the cold cement slab in his thin jacket with his arms around himself, wondering why in the world he was sitting there, waiting for a crazy old black woman.

This was just one of many things that his young mind could not figure out. For instance,

Jason was completely baffled by his mother's behavior, why she stayed with Billy, why she allowed him to do the things he did to her, his little sister and himself.

Last night, about eleven o'clock, Billy had come stumbling in, drunk as a lord, and yelling for his supper. Jason and his nine-year-old sister, Dodie, were asleep in their room in the small, four-room apartment. They woke up and Dodie threw her covers off and jumped out of her little twin bed. She ran softly across the floor and climbed into Jason's bed, cuddling as close to him as she could. Billy scared her, even when he wasn't drinking. They heard something crash and Billy curse. Their mother murmured something softly to calm him down, then came the sound of a thump and a smothered whimper.

As the racket in the living room continued, waxing and waning in volume, Jason found himself getting angrier and angrier. Why did his little sister have to hide in his bed? Why did his mother have to keep this miserable s.o.b. happy? Why did he, Jason, have to live like this, always dodging the back of Billy's hand?

Jason quietly got up and rummaged under his bed; he was looking for his baseball bat. He'd had to hide everything he loved from that crazy man, just another reason to hate him. His searching hands found what they wanted. Jason, dressed in his pajamas, and armed with the bat, burst into the battle ground. His mother was sitting at the table in the dining area of the small apartment, her hand over her left eye. Billy was standing over her, screaming unintelligible insults at her. Occasionally, here and there, Jason picked up words like "whore," "slut," and "useless sow."

Jason, inflamed with rage, ran like a berserker into the room, and hit Billy with the bat right smack in the kidneys. Billy went down with a howl.

Just then, there was a knock on the door. It was the apartment manager responding to neighbors whose sleep had been interrupted. Jason's mother went to the door. The manager, a fat little white woman in her sixties, said, "Miz Anglethwaite, you know I've had to tell you before, and I really like you and them kids, but, Miz Anglethwaite, I don't know how much longer we kin take Mr. Callahan's carryin' on. Next time, I'm not comin' up here, I'm callin' the po-lees.

"I'm sorry, Mrs. Kincannon, it's really nothin'. We'll be quieter." The ugly bruise beginning to form around her left cheek and eye belied his mother's soothing tones, smiling face.

Billy roused himself and rolled over onto an elbow. "You jus' go and call the po-lees, Miz

Kincannon. I wanna make a complaint. This here juvenile delinquent hit me with somethin' and I want him arrested. You hear that, you little bastard?" he screamed. "I'm gonna put your little ass in jail. See how you like that." Billy would not raise a hand to him or anybody as long as Mrs. Kincannon could see, Jason knew that. He also knew that when she was gone it was going to be Katie-bar-the-door time.

"Come on, Mom," he said. "Come on, we don't have to stay here. I'll go get Dodie, and we'll get outta here. Come on, Mom."

Billy staggered to his feet, left hand still on his back. "Listen, you li'l snotnose, I'm the man in this house, and I say who comes and who goes, and you're goin'. Ever'body else stays, you go. No little punk 'thout a beard is givin' orders around here. You li'l asshole," he said, advancing menacingly in Jason's direction. "My ol' man didn't taken no shit off punks, and neither do I, you hear me? Neither do I."

Jason ran into his bedroom and shut the door. "Get up, Dodie, get up," he said, pulling the covers back from his sister. His frantic behavior frightened her even more, and she clung to the covers, tears rolling down her little face. Jason was throwing clothes out of the chest-of-drawers onto the bed, flinging shoes and toys out of the bottom of the closet in his search for a suitcase. Through the door, Jason could hear Billy cursing and his mother sobbing and pleading in muffled tones. He heard a chair turn over as Billy went into his destructive mode; he could never be satisfied with just busting up furniture, though; he always had to bust up people, too. He was just getting a good head of steam on, and Jason knew he had to move pretty fast to get out of the line of fire. As he dressed, he tried to marshal his arguments, however he could convince his mother to pack up little Dodie and bring her so they could all escape. Then Billy burst through the door as Jason was tying one of his sneakers.

Billy, in his drunken anger, tripped on a half-completed model car. It was one of Jason's favorites, a 1958 Chevrolet Corvette. He would save working on it to reward himself in the evening when he had finished his homework. Unhappily, he had not been able to get at it for a while, between watching Dodie for his mom, and a thousand-and-one other things that seemed to prevent him from doing what he wanted for himself. Now, he never would work on it again. Billy picked it up and crushed in one ham fist. While he mourned the loss of his favorite model car, the upside was that this distraction gave Jason just the margin of time he needed. In almost one motion, Jason had his windbreaker and scooted out the bedroom door, right out under Billy's flailing arms, through the living room and into the street. He ran until he was out of breath, and then, seeing a bus loaded with employees from Barnes-Jewish Hospital on their way home, flagged it down at the bus stop.

He had managed to squirrel away a nice little cache from his odd jobs for neighbors and one of his teachers (hard to do with Billy around), but he had not had time to get it out of its hiding place. Nevertheless, he had stuffed a few dollars into his jeans pocket earlier in the day and this was what he brought out now and used for bus fare. He prayed that Billy did not go through the bedroom he shared with Dodie and find the money. As he counted out his fare his mind was on his little stash, his sister and his mother, all the things that he had left behind to Billy's dubious mercies. The bus driver looked at him oddly, but said nothing.

When they got downtown, he was the last one on the bus. The driver, a young man in his thirties, looked up at Jason and said, "Li'l man, this is the end of the line and I'm goin' to the garage now. You got folks gonna meet you, or what?" Jason said nothing, just fled through the open door into the shadows of an alley.

It was sleeting, with strong gusts of wind, but he didn't notice until he began to slow down and assess his situation. It was after midnight, and he was alone on a downtown street with no place to go, and the weather was terrible. He wasn't gonna cry, dammit, he wasn't gonna do it. He knew he could go to the police, and they'd either make Billy let him back in or they'd put him in Juvie. Neither prospect was attractive.

Once or twice the police had come to their apartment, after the neighbors had enough, and once even a social worker from the State of Missouri had come, in response to an anonymous complaint about the kids. She had separated everybody and questioned Dodie and Jason each alone. Their mother kept smiling nervously and making coffee. Billy stumbled all over himself, offering chairs and compliments (inside himself Jason had laughed at this; he knew how Billy hated blacks – "Can't no decent white man git nothin', they givin' it all to the niggers" - and this social worker was proudly, militantly black). Jason's answers to the social worker's questions were minimal. He would not do anything to hurt or embarrass his mom; she had enough to deal with.

After the social worker was gone, he prayed that she would come back unexpectedly to see for herself. That way, they could be rescued and Jason wouldn't have to rat on anybody. Of course, it never happened and Jason gave up praying. When he found out that the social worker's report had glossed over the complaint as "a bit of an exaggeration; the children are fed and clothed, they apparently attend school regularly" and "it is always in the State's interest to keep a family together, breaking it up as a last resort," he decided that God was his enemy, or maybe just a fiction. Either way, there was no use trying to get His attention.

When Anna Lee called to him out of the darkness he was emotionally anesthetized. He had learned some time ago that the best way to get through a crisis was not to feel it, just to keep focused on survival. He also hated this response in himself because it made him indifferent to his mom and to Dodie for whom he felt responsibility. He had been, after all, the man of the family until Mom took up with Billy.

He could barely remember his father, who had left when Dodie was only three months in the oven. Then, when Dodie was two and Jason five, Billy had come around, sweet-talkin' everybody and actin' like he cared what happened to 'em. The funny thing, though, was that he seemed to be unemployed a lot. Mom worked regularly on an assembly line at an electronics factory. She never made more than nine or ten dollars an hour, but somehow they got along. She was always tired, always broke, but she loved her children.

Jason was only five years old, but he understood that his mom was lonely and needed somebody. He tried his best to help take care of Dodie so Mom wouldn't have to worry too much, so at first Billy looked like a real blessing. When he wasn't working (which was a lot), he said he could look after the kids, be there when Jason got back from school, and Dodie didn't have to go to daycare, which was pretty expensive anyway. This looked like a real relief to Mom. It wasn't long, though, before Jason began to realize the truth of the maxim that all that glitters is not gold. He had come home several times from school and found Dodie unattended, Billy snoring on the couch with the vodka bottle dribbling its dregs onto the floor. One time, when Billy was unconscious, Jason found Dodie in the kitchen attempting to fix herself something to eat, standing on a chair at the gas stove, her little shirt sleeve catching fire. Jason threw a glass of water onto her arm before any major damage was done, however, the terrified screaming woke Billy who staggered into the kitchen and cuffed them both for disturbing him.

After a while, Jason began to understand that what was wrong with Billy was connected with the bottles he kept all the time. And pretty soon Billy was drunk daily, instead of two or three times a week. He just laid around the house in a stupor, only roused when something annoyed him, forcing him back into reality. Periodically, he went to a nearby neighborhood tavern and spent the evening. Once or twice he had been thrown out for fighting. He also occasionally worked as a day laborer for an agency that hired out on a daily basis, but he had nothing permanent in his life except for Jason, Dodie and their mother.

    Sometimes when Jason got home from school he'd start cleaning the kitchen so that his mom would have a little less to do when she got home; Billy would come in and sit at the kitchen table and stare at him. Jason didn't like this, but he said nothing, trying not to further annoy him. Billy would start mumbling about fathers and sons, how Jason was now his son and he would have to do as he was told. Billy would talk about his father, how his father had once broken his fingers for talking back to him, how his father had been undisputed king of his castle, and that was the way things should be. His mother had known her place, by God, and nobody back-talked the old man. He worked a full day and when he came home, dinner was on the table, the beer was in the refrigerator, and that was just plain that. Billy expected his home to be run the same way and, by God, it would, and no runt of a ten-year-old (or however old Jason was at the time) was gonna make it any different. Jason learned quickly enough that if he just let Billy talk, sooner or later he'd wander back to the couch and pass out and then Jason could get out his books and start his homework, assuming Dodie wasn't demanding attention. Then he'd have to get her occupied so he could get to his studies.

He finally started complaining to his mother after about two years of this routine, but his mother brushed him off, saying, "If I don't keep him around, who'll be here with you and Dodie? Anyway, honey, the only thing that's wrong with 'im is that he just drinks a little too much once in a while. All that'll change once he gets settled into a steady job."

"But, Mom," Jason protested, "He ain't even lookin' for a job. He just lays around here if the day labor don't call 'im."

"Jace, honey, how can you know? You ain't here durin' the day. That man's bustin' his bee-hind, tryin' to get work. He's jus' had some real bad luck lately. Everybody has bad luck sometimes. That's when they really need patience and understanding."

Jason knew better; but he saw there was no

use arguing with his mom, so he just let it go. He knew that sooner or later things would reach critical mass and something would change. He just didn't know what, and contemplation of the possibilities was terrifying.

After a while, Billy settled in. When his confidence in his place there with the Anglethwaites solidified, he started hitting people, notably Jason's mom. He started with the littlest, Dodie. Dodie was six years old and remarkably beautiful. She was also bright and charming and always teacher's pet in school because she was so responsive. Dodie thrived on praise; she needed it the way she needed food, water and air. She seemed to have been born with that need, along with a very low tolerance for discomfort. One day she was showing Jason a gold star she had earned at school. Billy lumbered into the kitchen and, bracing his arms on the table, blearily looked at Dodie. Without warning, he grabbed the paper with the star, crumpled it up and threw it into the trash can.

"What makes you think you're so hot, you little shit? Is it gold stars? Huh?" He grabbed Dodie's arm and jerked her across the table; she was small boned and light.

She was startled and began to cry, enraged at this insult to her dignity. She looked Billy right in the eye, little face red and tear-streaked, and screamed, "You drunk, you let me go." Billy backhanded her so hard that she lay on the floor without moving for several terrible seconds. Jason, his heart in his throat, bent over her.

"Get away from the little bitch," Billy shouted. "She don't need nothin' but a good lickin' on a reg'lar basis."

Jason just ignored him, feeling on her chest for her heart. He was terrified. He knew that this was just the beginning. He also knew that Billy in his drunken way was very cunning. He had isolated the single most vulnerable part of Dodie's character and unerringly wounded it. Jason's heart went from his throat into his shoes. He knew that he, as Dodie's big brother, had to do something.

He began doing odd jobs around the neighborhood whenever he could. Between keeping up with his schoolwork, trying to help his mom, protect his little sister and trying to make some money, he was a little boy on a merry-go-round, spinning at top speed toward disaster. He was hanging on for dear life, trying to keep his balance. His schoolwork began falling behind, and he was getting very cranky with his school mates. On the playground he started isolating, not wanting to play, just walking around the perimeters, hands in his pockets, staring at his shoes.

His teacher, Mrs. Lewison, noticed. She had watched Jason for five years, having spoken to him on the playground and in the cafeteria. She had always known that things were not exactly right in Jason's home. Unfortunately, her hands were tied. The sovereign state of Missouri had more laws on the books to protect abused animals than abused children. She had no evidence that Jason was in a bad environment; she had never found any bruises on him, he wasn't undernourished, and he generally made it to school, even with the occasional sniffle. Finally, she had made an anonymous call to the child abuse hotline. That was when the social worker came around and did nothing except make Jason hope, a hope that was quickly smothered and corroborated his growing suspicion that hope was a dangerous thing.

One morning at recess, Jason got into a fight, a real, honest-to-god fist fight. Mrs. Lewison was appalled, not only at the savagery with which Jason waded into his adversary, but it was simply so unlike him. After school in detention she tried to draw him out, but Jason refused to be drawn. Then she asked him would he like to do some yard work at her house the following Saturday. The change in him was astonishing.

"Mrs. Lewison, I can do lots of stuff, and I

come cheap, 'cause I need to watch my little sister. Is it okay if I bring Dodie?"

"Of course, Jason, I know Dodie. She's in Miss Sanders' third grade class, isn't she? Everybody knows Dodie. Miss Sanders says she's her best reader, maybe the best reader in the school," Mrs. Lewison smiled. She had made a breakthrough.

The following Saturday morning, Jason and Dodie were on her front stoop at eleven o'clock. The Lewison house was typical of the area: older, narrow, at least two-storey, small front yard, small backyard, all immaculately kept. As he and Dodie went up the steps of the front stoop, Jason looked around and could not see where there would be a lot of work to do, but oh, well. He twisted the bell knob under the large, oval-shaped beveled glass that occupied most of the front door. When Mrs. Lewison opened the door, he apologized, saying that he hadn't been able to get away any earlier. He didn't tell her that he'd had to sneak out while Billy was snoring on the couch and his mother at the grocery store. He'd left his mom a note, just saying that he was helping his teacher today. The less Billy could find out, the better. Most importantly, he should never know that Jason had any kind of income. He had once broken Jason's little fire engine bank when Jason had refused to give him the key. Billy had thrown it on the floor after first throwing Jason on the floor, and taken the entire stash of his hard-earned money. That was to be his, his mom's and Dodie's gettin'-away money, and it all went to feed Billy's raging disease.

Mrs. Lewison smiled and brought them both into the house and back to the backyard. She pointed to the old frame white-washed garage and said, "There are gardening tools in there, Jason. I need you to rake out the flower beds by the fences, and then spread the leaves out evenly so that they protect the bulbs that I put in."

Jason first settled Dodie on the back porch so she could be close to him while he worked. She had her little battered pink suitcase, filled with Barbie dolls and accessories and some story books. She sat on the wooden back porch steps in the fall sunshine and chattered to herself and her Barbies, occasionally reading to them from the books.

Jason worked like a demon in the small back yard, determined to do a good job; he cut grass, trimmed hedges and walkways, swept cuttings, raked and weeded. As small as it was, there was enough work to keep him busy for quite a while. The flowerbeds that were Mrs. Lewison's pride were against the fences separating the yard from those of the neighbors on either side, and he carefully raked and piled leaves onto the depressions that he knew meant bulbs had recently been put in. The dumpster was in the alley next to the alley entrance to the garage. A tall wooden gate let out to the alley, and he carried bags of leaves that he didn't use to the dumpster. He managed to master the trick of holding the lid open (the opening on top was about even with his eyes) while slinging the big green plastic bags of leaves inside. About three o'clock Mrs. Lewison called them into the kitchen, setting out glasses of milk and thick slices of chocolate cake. Dodie was ready to dive in, but Jason hesitated. His appetite had been poor of late; symptomatic of the depression that was stealing his soul.

"What's wrong, Jason, you don't like chocolate cake?" asked Mrs. Lewison.

"He loves it, he's just bein' stupid," said Dodie, between chews.

"Shut up, Dodie. When I need your help, I'll ask for it," Jason said. "I like chocolate cake, Mrs. Lewison, in fact, I love it. I jes', I dunno, I'm sorry. I'm fine, here, gimme that," he said, and grabbed Dodie's napkin and wiped her mouth. He then attacked the cake with gusto. He didn't want Mrs. Lewison to think he was ungrateful.

Margaret Lewison watched all this with some interest. There was that about Jason which touched her; perhaps it was the resemblance to her little Robbie, taken many years ago by spinal meningitis. Whatever it was, this young man moved her and she was most interested in his welfare.

"So, tell me, Jason," she said (got to move slowly here, can't risk losing him), "How's school been so far this year?" It was a fine day in late October, and the school year was still relatively young.

He washed down a mouthful of cake with milk, the residue around his mouth delineating the fine silky hairs there into a white mustache. He wiped it dry and said, "It's been fine Mrs. Lewison, just fine. This is really good cake. Thanks a lot."

"Do you think you would like to help me out on Saturdays all the time? It would be such a help to me and Mr. Lewison would be free to do some other things that he likes," she said. If she could just give Jason some idea that there was hope for a better life than the one he was currently living.

He paused, then said slowly, "Yeah, I'd like that, Mrs. Lewison, but sometimes it's hard for me to get away." He didn't want to tell her that he had to work everything around Billy. If

Billy ever found out that he was doing this, he'd come around and drag Jason and Dodie back to the apartment, embarrassing Jason beyond redemption with his drunkenness. And if he found out Mrs. Lewison was paying Jason, God only knew what kind of hell would break loose.

"Well, Jason, it's no big deal, but if you can arrange it, I sure would appreciate it." She didn't want to press too hard, knowing that Jason would withdraw if she did. She watched Jason's face closely. Margaret Lewison's mother had lived through Hitler's death camps, and, on her father's side, her people were Russian Jews. They had seen many a pogrom, and fear was their constant companion until the prayers for the dead were said over them. Even here, in the heartland of the United States, those who had known that kind of persecution never really felt safe. Margaret Lewison knew anxiety when she saw it, the habitual tic of looking over the shoulder. Jason had the look of someone who was pursued. Margaret looked at him, his slender body, his solemn eyes, and longed to hold him, stroke his hair. Oh, God, he looked like Robbie. Her arms ached to enfold him.

"Okay, Jason, what do I owe you?" she asked, getting her pocketbook out of her bedroom. She pulled out her wallet and handed him a twenty-dollar bill. "Is this about right?"

Jason gawped at the money, astonished. He had expected five, ten dollars, tops. This was largesse beyond his wildest dreams. "Oh, wow, Mrs. Lewison! That's too much." He looked distressed and rummaged in his pockets. He pulled from his jacket the little change he had brought to take himself and Dodie to the Dairy Queen on the way home. "I don't have enough change for that," he said.

"I don't want any change, Jason. You worked hard for four hours, and at five dollars an hour, I would say you earned it."

Jason stammered an embarrassed thanks, wiped Dodie's mouth and then returned to the back porch with her to help her gather up all her Barbie dolls and accoutrements.

After they had gone, Margaret Lewison sat at the kitchen table, just looking at the plates with crumbs, the empty glasses that had held milk. Lord, how she missed hearing the screen door slam and somebody yell, "Mom." Her other son and daughter were grown, with families of their own. Who knew what Robbie would have done. Maybe he would have been a rabbi.

Nevertheless, her child-rearing days were over and she knew it. She and Fred had already planned their retirement, down to the Winnebago and the trips with the grandkids. But she could not escape the feeling that she still had one more shot in her, and maybe Jason was it.

She shook her head, this was silly. She was fifty-two years old, she had not a leg to stand on, she could never get Jason in a court of law. But she knew she could offer Jason hope, and she would do it if it killed her. Somehow, she was going to show Jason that there was another kind of life than the one he was living.

More than one of her colleagues had had run-ins with Billy over the years, embarrassing confrontations about ridiculous things. One time, unbeknownst to Jason's mother, Billy had come up to the school and demanded that Jason be allowed to come home. At that time, Dodie was in morning kindergarten. It was afternoon, and Billy said he had things to do and couldn't be mindin' no kids, he was a man and had things to do. The school officials were not about to release Jason to Billy's custody and a terrible scene ensued in the office.

That afternoon Jason was sent home with a note from the principal, stating that she needed a meeting with his mother. After ascertaining that Jason knew nothing about the reason for this request, Mrs. Anglethwaite wrote back that she couldn't afford the time off work, but she would be happy to talk on the phone or meet on a Saturday with the principal. Time and place were worked out, and a meeting took place the following Saturday afternoon. The results were not at all satisfactory to the principal, but again, the school had boundaries in which the law insisted it operate, and the principal was wary of exposing the school to unnecessary litigation. In fact, she had no hard evidence except Billy's occasional tilts at the school, but she was a woman with a lot of experience with children, and she knew that sooner or later this situation was going to explode. Usually, it was the children who absorbed the concussion.

Jason continued working at Mrs. Lewison's when he could and the tension at school eased some. He would talk to her, bring his little sister and, Margaret hoped, he was getting some respite from his home situation during the time he spent at her house. Fred seemed to enjoy the boy, and would show him all his fishing gear in the garage. He taught him the best bait for the various species of fresh-water fish native to the local rivers and lakes, and they began to make big plans about fishing in the springtime.

Jason never said anything, just went along with the game, but in his heart he never believed there would ever be any fishing. He knew that his life was just one big running wound, and these little times would soon, somehow, be brought to an end. Billy was out to get him and nobody stood in his corner to defend or support him, not even his mom.

The holidays came and Margaret began putting Jason to work inside the house, doing little things. She and Fred were reformed Jews, and enjoyed putting up a Christmas tree for the kids when they were little, and now the grandkids. So Jason and Dodie were invited to a tree-trimming party. Both the Lewison offspring and their families came and Jason saw what Christmas could be like. If anybody noticed that Christian children had to go to a Jewish home to find Christmas spirit they never said anything. Margaret simply hoped that these family experiences would give Jason enough encouragement to believe in a better life.

It would have broken her heart to know how much it hurt him, how much like an outsider he felt, and how defensive he felt about little Dodie, ready to protect her from any slight. Jason watched the loving camaraderie with the envy of someone who is forever barred from the good things in life. He tried to tell himself at first that, sure, he would have all this someday; and when he couldn't convince himself, he tried to believe that it wasn't so great after all. That didn't work, either. His spirit bled in silence, but he couldn't stop coming back. He hated himself for his weakness, wished he could just say "no, thanks" to Mrs. Lewison, and not have to watch them all having fun and a kinship he could never enter, no matter how hard he tried. But what the Lewisons offered was his only relief from life at home. Then, too, Dodie enjoyed it so much; Jason didn't have the heart to tell her that they were just charity cases being tolerated by good people who wanted to do the right thing.

Chapter Three

When Jason didn't appear in the classroom that January morning, Mrs. Lewison paid no attention at first. It was the beginning of the second flu season, coughs and sniffles were a way of life in the St. Louis school district at this time of year. What she could not know was that Lorraine Anglethwaite was sitting at her kitchen table, deep in unhappy thought. She had been up all night, unable to believe that her son was out there somewhere in a cold winter night without protection. She was afraid for him, and afraid of what she knew she had to do.

Billy came staggering into the small kitchen in his underwear and ruffled her hair. He would be briefly sober until the day's drinking began, she knew that.

"Hi, babe," he said.

She looked up at him, and, as if seeing him for the first time, thought what a repulsive sight he was, in his briefs and T-shirt. His jaw was covered with stubble, his eyes bloodshot and bleary, the bags under them puffy. Her fear dissolved as her determination strengthened with amazement that she could ever have wanted this man.

When she didn't answer his greeting, he tried again. "Hey, honey, cat got your tongue? I need some coffee, where'd you get that cup of coffee?"

Wordlessly, she got up and started the water for a cup of instant coffee for him. As she maintained her silence, he began to get uncomfortable, and when Billy was uncomfortable, he got belligerent

"What's the matter? You ain't goin' to work, babe?" He waited a bit, trying to sound her out.

"Hey, you ain't not speakin' to me on account of Jason, are ya?" He was very careful with both his speech and body language, because here was a situation in which he knew intuitively he had to tread lightly. Because he was not an introspective person (although he certainly had the intelligence; just not the guts), he pushed aside the strange feeling that the control of which he was so sure here in this small apartment seemed to be eroding. But, ignore it though he might, the discomfort that it brought was making itself felt, and the familiar edginess was rising to the surface. In the meantime, he tried to play it calm, with the wisdom that comes from experience.

"He'll be all right. I hate to tell you how many nights I'd spent on the street by the time I was his age, and look at me; I'm okay. In fact, it pro'ly did me some good, taught me to survive.

An' anyway, how comes you ain't at work?"

Billy had never been able to honestly probe the gigantic nightmare of terror that his entire childhood had been. So he always fell back on the fiction that abuse built character and self-reliance, not alienation and mistrust, something that he, like all drunks, tended to confuse with courage and independence; that his father's acts of drunken sadism were actually acts of love designed to make a man of him. And, of course, there was no way in the world he could begin to talk about the self-hatred, even if he had been able to acknowledge its presence. It flourished like a poisonous vine in his soul, reaching out to infect all who came within reach. Its seeds were already festering in Jason.

"Come on, Lo, baby. He'll be okay," he reached over to stroke her hair.

Lorraine drew back from his touch, and the violence which was always simmering in him boiled over. A man didn't need this kind of rejection in his own home, and he slapped her, hard. She fell sideways off the chair, and then just stayed seated on the floor, her back against the sink cabinet, hair falling into her face. When she finally looked up at Billy, it was with a hate that put a chill down his spine.

"You better wipe that look off your face, girl, if you know what's good for you," he hoped that the surprise and (What? Was it actually fear?) other feelings her silence and look aroused in him did not show in his voice. He thought he might have heard a quaver in it when he spoke, and it didn't do for a man to not be sure of his own authority.

"Ya know, Billy, you can slap me all you want, you can leave bruises and call me names, but there's still gonna be some big changes around here. The biggest one is, you're goin'. Oh, yes," she said in response to the stunned look on his face. "Oh, yes, Billy-O, you're goin'."

He strode around the table, arm raised to hit her again.

"Go ahead, big man, hit me again, but that don't change nothin'. 'Cause when you get done hittin', you gonna head for that vodka bottle. Then you gonna drink yourself into a stupor, and when you do, I'm gonna take Jason's baseball bat and work your kneecaps over. See, what's goin' on here, you stupid drunk, is that this stupid woman has suddenly come up a little smarter.

"So that means two things, you silly ass. First, you better get your stuff together and clear your behind out of my, yes, I said **MY** apartment. My name is on the lease, not yours, and I'm puttin' you out, I'm done with you. No more smackin' me around or yellin' at my kids.

"And second, I'm gonna hurt you, if you

don't; be sure that if you close your eyes in this apartment, you won't be the same man when you open 'em again. Who knows what I'll do to you. Oh, I ain't gonna kill ya, 'cause you ain't worth goin' to prison over. But I'm gonna hurt ya, Billy-O, so you better clear your ass out, 'cause I'm sure-god gonna get you if you don't, and leave you permanently damaged."

Two of the most terrifying things in the present situation for Billy were, first, the term of endearment, "Billy-O," something she had called him only in private moments. The second thing was that the angrier Lorraine became, the softer her voice got. Right now, she was at a whisper. Billy grew up with shouting, cursing, and broken furniture and that was the way he performed. This quiet, intense hatred was scary.

He watched her as she reached for the chair and used it to pull herself to her feet. He backed away a little when she was in a standing position, but she kept coming, until she was right in his face.

"Ya know, Billy, after you fell into bed last night and started your snorin', I went into the bathroom, and ya know what I seen in the mirror? Huh? Well, I'll tell ya, whether you wanna know or not. I seen my mama. My mama, who I'd vowed I'd never be like, and there she was lookin' at me right out of my own bathroom mirror. My daddy used to slap her around at least three times a week, sometimes because supper wa'n't there when he got home at midnight drunk, or because it was cold when he got home at midnight drunk, or because he didn't like the look of it, or maybe just 'cause he didn't like the look o' her. Whatever it was, he'd just take a notion, and that was that, he was gonna hit her 'til he felt better. I watched that for sixteen years, wishin' she'd do somethin', anything, that would make him stop: kill him, kill herself, even kill me, anything so I didn't have to watch no more.

"I cain't tell you the nights we run out into all kinds of weather, my mama holdin' me and my sister, runnin' in the rain, or snow, or cold, to a neighbor's or the pastor's or somebody. An' nobody did nothin'. Once we went to the sheriff's substation, and they just said that a man's home was his castle, and didn't nobody wanna interfere with a man in his own home, an' she jes' oughta stop aggervatin' him, and he'd stop hittin' her.

"One night, when I was sixteen years old, it was a Sattidy night, and it's when ever'body goes out, hellin' around in their hot cars and drinkin' in the taverns down there. Daddy come home and seen me gettin' ready for bed. I just come from work, and he come and stood in my bedroom door, all likkered up and smellin' somethin' awful, and tol' me what a purty gal I was, and how he didn't realize how much a woman I'd become, and the time was comin' when he had some things to show me about how a woman oughter 'preciate a man, 'specially if that man was her daddy who'd been supportin' her all these years.

"Well, Billy, I knew what that meant, cause down there, where I come from, that's a way of life, and I'd already seen what he'd done to my sister. So, the followin' week, when Vern come through in his big ol' eighteen-wheeler, and asked me to go with 'im, I went.

"See, Billy, my sister started drinkin' when she was fifteen, 'cause it helped get her through them Sattidy nights with our daddy. I was fourteen when we found her one Sunday mornin', dead from alcohol poisoning and some kinda pills she'd took.

"I wasn't about to do a rerun of that pitcher, so Vern didn't have to ask me twice. I got aboard Vern's rig, and away we went. I thought I'd escaped, Billy, 'cause see, while Vern was a drinker, too, he wa'n't violent. He'd just wander off and disappear for days.

"Then come the day when he wandered off and never showed up again. I had my two children, and, Billy, you may not believe this, but I love them kids. They're the only people in this world who ever loved me enough to die for me; I know my boy would. He was ready to do it last night, and I didn't do a thing to help him, and I'm ashamed.

"Ya know, he'd complained about you before, and I'd took your part against my little boy. Jes' like when I'd ask my mama why she didn't leave Daddy. I know now why she didn't: 'cause she didn't have nuthin' else. But I do, Billy, I do. Well, maybe I don't right now, but leastways I know how to get it. And when I looked in that bathroom mirror and seen my mama, I knew I had to do somethin' about gettin' it, or there wa'n't no point in goin' on." She shook her head and laughed a little ruefully. "I don't think I'd know what to do with a sober man; drunks is all I've ever known all my life. So I reckon the only thing left to do is jes' leave y'all alone, 'cause I sure cain't pick 'em, can I."

Billy was simply aghast at this speech. It was the most words he'd ever heard Lorraine string together at one time. He'd had no idea what her childhood had been like, and, truth to tell, he was never interested enough to ask her. He did know that she hailed from Hayti (she pronounced it Hay-tie), Missouri, that she'd quit school to work in a truck stop and married Vernon Anglethwaite, a truck driver who'd deserted her when she was pregnant with Dodie.

That, however, was information that she had volunteered, and had nothing to do with his needs, therefore, was of no interest to him.

This was simply not the Lorraine he knew; he'd never seen her angry, never heard her raise her voice, or worse, go into this terrible hoarse whispering, which spoke of an old and dangerous rage. He had to reassert himself; he had to get things back to where they had been.

He opened his mouth, but she cut him off. "Now, Billy-O, you have exactly nine minutes before I call the po-lees. I'm callin' at nine-thirty to talk about my boy, and what you done last night. If I was you, I'd clear out. And don't ever come near me, my children or this apartment again."

She walked out of the kitchen into the living room, and sat down on the couch by the telephone to watch the clock tick off the minutes.

After an eternity reckoned by Jason's young hungry clock, Anna Lee came back. She had wrapped in a napkin some toast and fruit, and a small carton of milk.

"Here," she said, thrusting it at him. "You eat up, and then you're gonna tell me how come you to be out in the middle of the night."

Jason gratefully grabbed the food and hugged his jacket around himself. The wind is sharp in downtown St. Louis; sometimes the wind whipping through those downtown canyons in January could be rougher than a winter walk on Chicago's Lake Shore Drive.

Anna Lee put her arm around him and walked him down the alley so that they wouldn't have to pass Father Leon's door. Anna Lee knew that Father Leon would ask a lot of questions that she wasn't prepared to answer at this point. Right now, this boy needed attention, and Anna Lee didn't want any interference. Later on, down the road, maybe she'd come to Leon for advice, but right now, she had some nurturing to do.

When they got back to her place by the air turnaround, they sat down. Anna Lee kept her arm around him, to shield him from the chill. He ate, gulped down his milk, and then looked up at her.

"Thanks a lot. Ya know, ya really didn't have to do all this." He could not believe that somebody would go to all this trouble for him. He hadn't had this kind of attention from his mother since Billy moved in.

"That's okay, boy. Now, you tell Anna Lee everything. Don't leave anything out."

"Well," he began, carefully choosing his words, "There really ain't all that much to tell. My stepdaddy, well, he ain't really my stepdaddy, 'cause he and my mom never got married, but anyway, Billy, that's his name, came home again last night drunk, and started smackin' my mom around. I guess, I dunno, I just got so tired of it all."

He shook his head, blond hair blowing, looking down at the napkin that he'd used to wipe his hands. He didn't want to tell Anna Lee how he felt he'd failed both his mother and his little sister by not staying there and having it out with Billy. It never once entered his little-boy mind that a grown man would have had second thoughts about dealing with Billy without some kind of backup. All Jason knew of life outside the apartment was the cartoons and Arnold Schwarznegger movies that helped him escape, filled with impossible heroes doing impossible things. Nobody understood the shame he felt at his inability to vanquish the one and only real bad guy he'd ever known. Not only had he run, but he had left the two women in his life in the hands of the enemy. It just seemed that, no matter how hard he tried, things just kept deteriorating. He didn't seem to have enough fingers to plug all the holes in his dike, and it was crumbling.

Anna Lee looked at him. She pulled an old muffler out of her jacket, that wonderful voluminous jacket, with all kinds of hidden pockets. She had begged it off the Salvation

Army, where it had been left by a Viet Nam vet who, after twenty years of life on the street, had killed himself. She wrapped it around Jason's head, who moved and objected to it.

"Hush, now, boy. Don't you know that ninety percent of your body heat escapes through your head? I'm not tryin' to embarrass you, I'm tryin' to keep you healthy. We'll get you some kind of real hat here in a bit. But while you're just sittin' here, not movin', you need somethin' to keep you warm.

"So, this Billy person, he run you off?"

"Yes ma'm."

"Well, who's your legal guardian? Where's your daddy?"

"My daddy left when I was small, I hardly 'member 'im."

"So all you got is your mama, and who else?"

"Dodie, that's my little sister."

"Well, Jason, just for now, let's not worry about it. I know that a boy your age ought to be in school, but maybe we'll just let you have a little vacation for a coupla days, here with Anna Lee. The thing is, we'll have to be careful, 'cause the authorities, they see you down here, and you're as good as in Juvie, you see what I'm sayin'?"

"Yes ma'm, I see, and don't think I'm not

grateful, but, you know, I'm worried about Mom and Dodie."

"And you don't think you're responsible for your mother and little sister, do you?" Jason looked down, ashamed of running off instead of standing up to Billy.

"Boy, you look here at Anna Lee." She tilted his chin up toward her face. "Now just what I said is what's gonna happen: you're gonna have a little rest here with me for a bit, and then we'll talk to Father Leon about all this. You'll see, it'll be okay. But until I tell you, don't say anything to anybody, and try to not be seen. There're those that think they've got a duty to tell everybody's business, and we're not ready to talk yet.

"There is one thing you gotta know, though, and that's that…," here she paused, uncertain as to how to continue. Anna Lee had not had a lot of practice in her latter years talking to rational people. She occasionally talked to the mission people, like Father Leon, but that was brief and only when necessary. She did not know how to explain to Jason about her schizophrenia. "See, Jason, it's like this. I have these bad spells, where I forget where I am, even who I am. I might disappear even for a couple of days. Generally, I can feel 'em comin' on, and if I feel one, I'll sure warn you. In that case, you go straight to Father Leon. He'll be able to help you, and keep you safe. You understand? You don't ever run these streets unless I'm here to take care of you. This is really important."

The urgency in her face startled Jason, so he just said, "Yes, ma'm," and didn't ask any questions. Father Leon it would be, just out of respect to this strange, large black woman, who seemed so gentle, no matter how odd.

The knock at the door came just as Lorraine Anglethwaite was pulling her sweatshirt over her head. Good, they'd come pretty quick. She opened the door to two uniforms, one of whom was Sean Patrick O'Herlihy. Sean was suffering from a monumental hangover and was in no mood to fool with hysterical women. Damn these women, think that they can just snap their fingers and you'll be there to clean up the mess. Drain the juices out of you, and cut you loose. Well, here was one Irishman that wasn't about to take that kinda shit off anybody; battle lines were drawn, 'cause ya hadda take a stand.

His partner, Wilson S. Phillips, was a large friendly black man, who seemed to deal well with people. He and Sean did not get along, so they seldom talked. Sean didn't have a lot of use for persons of African descent in general anyway, and while he never said as much,

Phillips was not bereft of insight. They were stuck with each other, and so be it. Phillips did not care to think what might happen if an actual crime should occur and he needed his back covered. Even if Sean didn't hate him for being black, he would probably be too drunk or shaky to be of any use. So Phillips didn't think about it; instead he just regularly put in for transfers to different divisions. He knew that sooner or later, somebody would pick him up, and he'd be free of Sean. In the meantime, he would do what he had to do to live with the situation.

Lorraine opened the door and invited the men in for coffee. Sean saw the shabby sofa, the coffee table overturned, and the alcohol stains on the rug. He had vaguely remembered being called here once before, a couple of years ago, for domestic disturbance.

Dodie peeked out her bedroom door and then came out and stood by her mother, looking wide-eyed at the two policemen. Lorraine absently patted her, reassuring, and kept measuring out instant coffee for the boiling water.

Phillips said, "None for me, ma'm. I've had four cups already, and that's two over my limit. Thanks anyway."

Sean sat down at the kitchen table, notebook open. Lorraine quietly told the essentials of what had happened the night before, focused largely on Jason and his flight. It was cold out there, and she was worried. Phillips asked her about Billy, where he was and did she want to press charges. She indicated that she didn't know, but suspected he had gone to his mother's house. She really wasn't interested in Billy's whereabouts anyway. All she wanted was her boy back, safe.

Sean took down the description of Jason, and looked at his latest school picture. He said nothing, but Phillips knew that as soon as they got back into the cruiser, he'd start mumbling about faithless women, "two-holers" he called them. Phillips had never seen a man so bitter about women. Sean had been divorced two years ago from the mother of his only son, Sean Michael. The ex-Mrs. O'Herlihy had finally gotten enough of his drinking binges, irregular cop hours, and all the other instability that comes with the territory of law enforcement and heavy drinking, and put him out. She had then gotten herself a truly savvy attorney, a man who had been through two divorces himself, and had taken a significant bite out of Sean's paycheck.

Between child support and alimony, Sean could hardly support his drinking. Money was hoarded for benders, which lately had been increasing in frequency and length. His bitterness had likewise grown commensurately. Sean felt endlessly sorry for himself, and was angry with everyone. Phillips didn't even tell him to hush; he just kept to himself and prayed for speedy deliverance to another division.

Sure enough, when they got back into the cruiser, Phillips took the wheel and Sean started muttering to himself. He seldom addressed any comments directly to Phillips, and the latter was grateful for that. He could just hear pieces and bits of Sean's monologue, bitterly complaining about his powerlessness over his life, the raw deal he had gotten, etc., and so on and on and on. This time, however, there was a break in the pattern.

"Hey, Phillips," said Sean, looking directly at him, "You got kids. My boy's about ten now. Where do you suppose a kid his age could go and spend the night?"

Phillips was startled. Here was Sean, actually thinking about something other than his own misery. "I dunno. We could look in alleys and like that, but I don't have a clue."

Father Leon Devereux was sitting at his desk in his little office, working on the books, doggedly trying to make less money turn into more money. While the United Way, Catholic Charities and some government subsidies helped,

Leon depended largely on individual donations. The large donors, like Anheuser-Busch Brewery, were generous, however, there just weren't that many like that around, and an operation like Leon's, small as it was, was costly. There were hidden expenses that were unpredictable: medical costs for sick people who staggered in; better nutrition, like fresh fruits and vegetables, which have a very brief shelf life. Sometimes, when he felt it was a good risk, he would go somebody's bail, and occasionally he had been stung, money lost.

Frequently, the notorious St. Louis weather would cause numerous casualties. During the winter, it was not unheard of here for the mercury to plummet to minus ten degrees Fahrenheit, with wind chills up to minus fifty. When his beds filled up, he would have to distribute thermal blankets, caps, gloves and socks to prevent frostbite on the passed-out drunks who slept in the alleyway and little courtyard around his place. These people depended on him, and he hated to fail them, more than anything.

Then, again, during the summers here, his food expenses went up right with the thermometer, especially during July and August, when the mercury seemed stuck between 95° and 100°. The dumpsters where the homeless normally prowled could not keep the refuse in a usable state, so they had to come into the missions and shelters for more food. Weather was a powerful and unstable factor in his financial prognostications; he never knew when he would have to yell "help" for emergency shortages.

As he sat there at his old, scarred desk and struggled to make the ends of the month meet, it never occurred to him, nor would it ever, that he could have done something less frustrating with his life. He had known since he was very young that he must serve his God in a meaningful way. Distractions had been many and a couple of them had been mesmerizing, but now that he was here, on the Row, serving the unloved, unwanted and unwashed, and he was as happy as if he had good sense.

He looked up at a faint rustle to see Frank O'Meara lounging in his office door, hat pushed back on his head, hands warming up as they surrounded a thick white mug of coffee from the perpetual urn in the kitchen.

"Hey, Lee," Frank said, looking around and shaking his head in mock disgust, "When you gonna get some decent furniture in here? This place always looks like a damn rummage sale."

"Frank, have you nothing better to do than

come in here and put the knock on my lovely decor? Has the city finally run out of criminals that my tax dollars should be paying for you to come in here and suck up my free coffee?"

Leon looked up at Frank, turning in his old-fashioned swivel desk chair. Actually, he had acquired both the desk and chair at a rummage sale, and what they lacked in esthetic appeal they made up for in sturdiness. Of course, Frank knew exactly where they had come from, but insulting remarks were part of the greeting ritual between them. Their friendship was a balance of cynicism and idealism. Both men knew that they had chosen lives which operated on the fringes of polite society; each sought in his own way to keep chaos from having the final say.

"Don't try to hand me that pious twaddle, St. Leon, patron saint of the chiselers. I happen to know that you got one of the best scams goin' here, with all your nonprofit disclaimers and exemptions and et cetera and so forth. You ain't paid a nickel's wortha tax since the Great Flood."

"Ah, but Frank, where else could you swill down gallons of free coffee and hide from the outlaws if I didn't have this wonderful shelter? Who would tolerate your execrable chess playing? Your endless complaints? Who but my sainted self? And sainted I will certainly be when the Vatican hears what I have endured at your hands. Surely your constant harassment qualifies as martyrdom."

Leon closed up his account books, grateful for the distraction Frank brought. He got up, put the books into the drawer and locked the desk with the little brass key.

"Now, who in the hell would be interested in that desk? Unless, of course, that's where you've stashed all the loot you're screwed out of an unsuspecting public."

Leon grinned at him, great, square, white teeth flashing in contrast to his dark African face, as he pocketed the keys in his black trousers. He went back into the kitchen to get himself a mug of steaming coffee, and then came back and joined Frank in the little sitting room off the office, part of his private quarters. This was where he wore his mantle of priesthood most lightly, in fact, where he most enjoyed it. Leon would always love being a priest, and he could never stop being one, even in his sleep. But here, in his little sanctuary, although his inner ear was always tuned to his Creator, he carried the load he so gladly shouldered much more lightly. Here he was a man with another man, thinking about very human things. The things that he shared with Frank, his own humanity, were allowed to live in here. And Leon was very human, indeed. He honored his humanity; it was another of

God's great gifts, and he always treated it that way, even when it burdened him.

The chessboard was exactly as it had been left two days ago, when Leon had stood up, yawned and stretched, looking at his watch and commenting on the late hour. So he said, "Time for a little R and R, wouldn't you say, Frank?"

Frank had already draped his coat over the arm of the saggy old couch, and propped his feet on a threadbare ottoman, waiting for Leon. Leon sat down at the chessboard. "Don't you want to play today?"

Frank said, "No, actually, I don't. I don't have a lot of time right now, just felt like a cup of your terrible coffee and the sight of your ugly mug."

Frank reached behind him and rubbed his hand across the small of his back, which was a little tired. What he didn't say, what he didn't know how to say, was that, once again, he had urinated bright blood that morning, and it was getting brighter and more frequent. It scared him, and, as always when he was scared, he had to examine the source of his fear in degrees; a direct approach to this thing was not possible.

Frank and Leon were approximately the same age, that is to say, in their early to middle fifties. Leon's health was considerably better, but then he had never abused himself as much as

Frank, nor did he live with the kind of tension that was a given in the life of law enforcement officers. They just sat there quietly as old friends can do, comfortable with each other and the silence between them.

"Hey, Lee, how long has it been since you practiced any real medicine?" Frank asked. He knew that Leon Devereux was an M.D., having come to St. Louis to study at the St. Louis University School of Medicine some years ago. What he didn't know was how to approach the subject of urinating blood without betraying that he was the one doing it.

Leon looked at him, surprised. Very seldom did the conversation take such a direct personal turn. Like most men, they displayed their affection for each other by respecting limits; respect had nurtured their friendship, and what they had learned about and from each other had come in the natural flow of conversation over the years.

"Well, it's been a while, Frank, and I can't honestly say I'm state-of-the-art anymore. What little I do is usually by way of just maintaining the status quo, rather than any real healing." His tone became cautious. "Is there anything specific I can tell you?"

Frank sighed. "No, I guess not. I was just bein' nosy, I guess. Part of a cop's nature, wantin' to know everything."

Leon folded his hands together in front of him, and leaned forward, his elbows on his knees. Leon, not being anything like a fool, knew that something was up here, something significant. He was going to have to walk very carefully in order to break down the barriers, even though he knew that Frank really did both want and need to talk.

"Frank, if there was ever anything I could do for you, I hope you know that I would gladly do it. I don't wish to be embarrassing, but I would think that by now you would know that you are more than just a casual friend to me, and anything that I have is yours for the asking."

Frank sighed again. This was so hard, but he knew that eventually the priest would pry it out of him; Leon was just too savvy to be put off with vague hand wavings. Not only that, he really wanted to tell Leon, it was just so difficult to get the first words out.

"Well, actually, Lee, I have been having a little problem lately, and I need to know if it's serious enough to see a professional."

He paused, looked at his hands, then directly at Leon. "I've been urinating blood. Not constantly, mind you, but mostly first pee, in the morning. Lately, it's been appearing at other times, too. Not always, but enough to get my attention, and I was wondering if this is symptomatic of anything meaningful, or just something that will pass, like some infection or something." As he spoke, his eyes slid away, while his voice and diction faded into a mumble, until the last part was almost inaudible.

Sensitive to Frank's embarrassment, Leon carefully chose his words. "I couldn't hear the last clearly, but I believe you indicated that your symptom is not diminishing, but, to the contrary, increasing.

"Blood in the urine is always symptomatic of something important, sometimes more, sometimes less, but always important. This could be indicative of anything from kidney stones to prostate cancer. At our age, Frank, prostate cancer is a risk. Furthermore, you and I are both celibate, I by choice, and you by circumstance. This always increases the risk. I would say, in fact, I implore you, please get some immediate medical attention. I don't have the facilities here to test you, or I would do it myself, but any doctor can see to it that you get them, and these days, it is possible to get results pretty quickly. Please, Frank, do it, just to stop us both from worrying."

Here Leon took a deep breath, and then the plunge: "Also, I am aware of how much you drink. What it's doing to your liver and kidneys is probably horrible. Simple abstinence may be all that you need."

He sighed and smiled self consciously. "I wouldn't dream of telling you what to do, Frank, just what I know."

Francis Xavier O'Meara, minion of the law, was fifty-five years old, two years older than Leon Devereux. He was the end of a long line of Irish Catholic alcoholics; alcoholism had killed his father, a gentle man whom Frank had loved very much. He hadn't been a mean drunk, just a quiet one. He had never been violent with his wife or children, but gradually became more and more inaccessible, until his heart gave out. This was just as well, because his liver was so cirrhotic that a lingering, terrible death was the only other option.

He had left a bewildered widow and three hurting children. Frank's sister, Teresa, was now a grandmother, and his brother, Kevin, had taken Holy Orders as a young man.

Frank had stopped going to church long ago. The God of his childhood had turned out to be stone-deaf, or so it seemed. He remembered praying to Him in times of crisis: during his father's last illness, when Alzheimer's ruined his mother, when his first partner was fighting for his last breath, and finally when his wife left him. In all cases, this God had failed him. Either He couldn't hear or He didn't care. Okay; this showed Frank that he could get along without Him, and he proceeded to do so.

His career in law enforcement buttressed this philosophy; he would look at the messes that fell to him to clean up, and know that there could not possibly be a loving and involved God. Over their endless chess game he had debated this point with Leon, then gone home to a tall tumbler of scotch whiskey. This was so he could get to sleep; otherwise, he would lie there and remember the faces, faces of suffering, confusion, hate and pain. Where was this all-powerful God then? The scotch blotted them out; it gave him a warm feeling going down, and dulled the sharp edges of a bitter reality. After a while, he found that he really needed to have this little nightly rite in order to sleep, and sometimes an ounce or two with dinner was a nice treat. He, like his father, was not a mean or noisy drunk. He just wanted some peace and quiet after a day of collecting human garbage, and he didn't see a thing wrong with that.

Frank and his ex-wife had never had any children. Sometimes he was glad of that, since they would have been the product of a broken home. Other times, he wished he'd had a son, a son to pass his wisdom on to, and a daughter to pamper. How he would have loved grandchildren! He always spent Thanksgiving and Christmas at Teresa's. There were her children and her children's children, and Kevin came, too. It seemed like every year, somebody had a new baby. He would sit quietly in the background with his drink. The combination of the whiskey and young life tumbling about him always gave him a glow. For a little while, the world was an orderly and hospitable place.

Chapter Four

Sean Patrick O'Herlihy was gloriously, spectacularly drunk. He was larger than life, and knew if he wanted to, he could leap tall buildings at a single bound. He was swapping war stories with the other uniforms who frequented Clancy's, making racist jokes. Here is where St. Louis' finest blew off steam, and thank God or somebody that such an outlet existed. The attitudes were anything but politically correct, and the policemen chose to segregate themselves, black from white. Here in Clancy's, this was a white hangout. Wilson S. Phillips, for example, would not be caught dead in here. Nobody would put him out if he walked in, but the silence as he was identified in the dim gloom, would be a powerful message, loud and clear. So here the white boys in uniform came, to vent their cynicism and reassure themselves that THEY were okay, even if the rest of the world was truly fucked up. Here is where they made their jokes about women, niggers, sheeny defense lawyers, the un-American American Civil Liberties Union and all the rest of the population who frustrated them.

But nobody could top Sean when it came to anti-female rhetoric. Most of his drinking buddies had an unspoken understanding that nobody was to get Sean started on the subject of women and their perfidy; he could and would hold forth for hours on this same topic, usually clearing the place out, until his face finally fell on the table, and drool slid out of the corner of his mouth. Then Luigi, owner and bartender extraordinaire (and the subject of quite a few jokes himself, considering his establishment was named "Clancy's." Many years prior he had purchased the bar from the original Clancy and decided it was good business not to change the name.) would have to bring him around and clean up his mess, along with the other closing-up chores. Luigi didn't mind this too much. Sean was a valued and free-spending customer, although of late, his tab was growing and payments diminishing.

Tonight, however, Sean left the subject of women alone, because he had his eye on a young female rookie who wore trousers well. Sean had spent the last week or so fantasizing about the contents of those trousers and what he would do if he could ever pry them off her. She was sitting quietly in a corner with a couple of other newbies, nursing a beer. She had looked his way several times, and each time she had smiled. Sean was encouraged; the smiles and the beer were turning him into a Smooth Operator, and he was strutting. Maybe he wouldn't have to go home alone tonight.

That was starting to be a problem, this going home alone, and he had begun closing up Clancy's several times a week to avoid it. The alcohol never gave good sleep. He would pass out and then wake up, his entire nervous system clanging in what oldtimers called the jitters. He couldn't get back to sleep, and would just lie there, ticking off the list of injustices that had been done him in his thirty-three years. He knew every one and enjoyed in a perverse way going over them all in detail. Finally, when the rage was out of control he would go to the kitchen and pop the top on a beer can, drain it, maybe add a second one, and return to unconsciousness. His father had done this, too. Neither one had ever heard the expression, "merry-go-round drinking," and would not have applied it to their own behavior if they had. Sean would think about every woman who had ever betrayed him, starting with his alcoholic mother who had abandoned him when he was three years of age.

He had been left with a father whose mood swings were manic. Nobody ever knew if the old man was actually a victim of bipolar disease, or if his substance abuse caused it. In the mornings, after a good drinking bout, he took dexies to get himself started, so his body chemistry was always yo-yoing. One night, in a fit of drunken melancholy, he shot himself dead.

Sean blamed his father's suicide not on booze and pills, but on his mother's betrayal. If she had stayed where she belonged, if she had been the right kind of woman who knew her place and her responsibilities, like the nuns who taught him and frequently punished him, his father would be alive; he would have had decent raising, they would have been a happy family. On account of her, he knew he was always searching for a mother, and could not relate to any of the tramps that he somehow always got involved with.

He just could not understand that: how could so many women appear so good and be such whores? It never entered his mind that the flaw was within him. If somehow he managed to connect with a moral woman, he hounded, importuned and threatened until he got her into bed; then he hated her for being easy.

Over and beyond that, these women of morality whom he found and seduced were generally rescuers, having had unhappy childhoods themselves, and were seeking to satisfy some strange need to combine rescue with romance. In their pain, they didn't understand that the one usually cancels out the other, and they would try to change Sean, save him from himself. In the process, they hoped that he would be grateful enough to love them.

They never succeeded, and healthy-minded women kept away from him. Usually, all he got was the periodic one night stand with a barfly. He had even occasionally coerced a lady of the night out of her services in exchange for not running her into the stationhouse. He considered this extremely clever on his part, and prided himself on never having had to buy sex.

Tonight, though, ha-HAH! Li'l Rookie Sweet Cheeks looked ripe for the pickin's, and he would be one first class picker. He turned to Luigi and said, "Hey, Lu, give the cutie-pie in the corner whatever she's drinkin' on me."

Luigi did so, adding the amount to Sean's tab. Sean looked into the corner when the beer was served and raised his bottle in smiling salute. She was sitting at a table with two male uniforms, a fair distance across the busy and raucous room. However, her eyes kept straying his way.

He made his way through the tables and pulled up a chair next to his prey. "Hiya, sugar buns. How long you been outta the academy?" He knew perfectly well, along with the rest of the department, that a class had just graduated, but he had to start the conversation somehow.

She smiled, and he noticed the deep dimple in her left cheek. Oh, God, she was too much; he wondered if her other cheeks were dimpled, too.

"I just graduated, this month."

"Who're you partnered with?"

One of the guys at the table looked at him coolly and said, "Me."

This startled Sean, and he realized, as he looked into Me's eyes, that he was being sized up and dismissed by a rookie. Furthermore, he knew that Me was lying to him. Newbies were never partnered together for all the obvious reasons. This infuriated him. Gotta go slowly here, don't wanna mess up with Miss Dimples.

He smiled, "Well, lucky you." He turned back to Dimples, smiled, and stuck out his hand. "I'm Patrolman Sean O'Herlihy. Maybe not a livin' legend yet, but I'm workin' on it."

She smiled back and said, "Rita Cavendish. I think I have heard of you. These are my friends, Ray Stillwater and Stan Olsen."

Sean just smiled and nodded, but did not extend his hand. Ray nodded back, without the smile. Okay, here we go. Sean could not figure out if Ray had some secret agenda, like he felt that Rita was his private property, or if he just didn't like Sean on sight. There were departmental rules about romance among the fraternity, but rules cannot control chemistry, so anything was possible.

Ray stood up, threw some bills on the table, and said, "I gotta go. You ready, guys?"

Rita looked up and said, "You know, I think I'll stay a while." Sean simply beamed at his good fortune.

Ray said, "Are you sure? We got roll call at 7:00 in the morning."

Rita said, "I'll be fine. I just wanna have a little relaxation after all the pressure and new stuff." She laughed a little self-consciously and said, "I'm startin' a whole new life here, Ray. I gotta test all the waters."

Ray looked hard at Sean, nodded, shrugged and stalked out the door.

Stan, the other rookie at the table, looked at Sean and Rita, and likewise stood up and made excuses. Good, thought Sean, a rookie who can take a hint. Now the road was clear, and he gathered up his forces to take a running shot at Rita.

While Frank O'Meara was at home, ruminating on calling a doctor, Leon Devereux feeding chicken broth to a sick drunk, and Sean O'Herlihy preening his feathers for Rita Cavendish, Anna Lee McIntosh was at the Rev. Joe Reis's shelter, looking for a cap for Jason. She was standing in front of Rev. Reis's desk, explaining to him what she wanted. "Reverend, I need a small cap, not big enough for me, it's for a small man."

"Well, Anna Lee, why can't he come get it himself? You know it's against the rules to just hand stuff out like that."

Anna Lee mentally planted herself. She hated a liar, and she hated to lie, but she knew that the truthful alternative could have bad results. "Reverend, this poor li'l man could hardly find his own backside, if he used both hands and hadda flashlight. I see 'im layin' in the alley all the time, breathin' hard, I don't even know 'is name, but I know he needs his head covered."

The Rev. Joe Reis knew very well that there were drunks who wanted nothing more than to be left alone while they waited for the end, which would be welcome. Until that came, their only interest was in avoiding sobriety as much as possible. There had been times when he'd had to forcibly put socks on some poor wetbrain with toes black from frostbite who just wanted to be left alone. While he knew that he couldn't stop them from drinking, nor the progress of the disease, his conscience insisted that they be made as comfortable as possible until alcohol poisoning, cirrhosis or exposure actually killed them.

He sighed and shifted his sizable girth in

his old desk chair. It had two arms and four wheels, and as he did so, the chair slid a little back, until it bumped into a small filing cabinet. Banging into things in his small office was a frequent event every day, so the Rev. Reis took no notice. Joe Reis was an ex-Marine. He had served in Viet Nam and knew more about the dark side of life than most people can imagine. He had learned the worst lesson that war can teach a man, and the one thing that no one ever wants to know: his own capacity for evil. His response to this information was to commit his life to a higher ideal. He diligently sought his Grail, but he always had one foot in the real world. Right now, he could smell something amiss; something in Anna Lee's body language betrayed her, although he could not precisely identify it. He had always liked Anna Lee, had always felt that she was something really special, maybe one of the "angels unawares" that Paul describes in Hebrews 13:2. Thus, it was not in his heart to deny her, but all of his alarm bells were certainly ringing as he sat here behind his old desk in the cluttered office of the shelter he ran, his hands folded across his generous belly. "Anna Lee, you sure you're tellin' me the truth?" Although he couldn't imagine the purpose of such a lie; why would she lie to him? He had always given her what she wanted, he had always trusted her, and oddly enough, even right now as he doubted her story, he was still sure that, whatever her purposes, Anna Lee was as trustworthy as they come.

Anna Lee looked him straight in the eye and said, "Rev. Reis, have you ever known me to try to run a game on you?"

He sighed again. "No, Anna Lee, I haven't. Okay, let's go to the wardrobe room, and we'll dig up what we can."

He heaved himself out of the old wooden chair and squeezed himself between it and battered, overflowing file cabinets just behind the desk. Only the Rev. Reis and God knew what he kept in there, and how he kept track of it. Even the help, both paid and volunteer, threw up their hands and rolled their eyes when they walked into his office. He didn't care. He knew it was mostly bills that would never get paid, promises of donations never made. He never worried about that too much, because his belief in his mission was unshakable. As he had learned to do first in Viet Nam, and then life in general, he just picked himself a path through the litter, avoiding teetering piles with the grace of a dancer, while pulling out his big keychain and fumbling for the right key to get Anna Lee's cap.

Anna Lee said nothing, but inside, she was jubilant. She knew she couldn't keep Jason, but while she had him, nobody was going to be able to say that she didn't take care of him. When they finally took him away from her, they were going to get him in as good a condition as she could arrange. She took the hat and went out into the dark evening.

    At six-thirty in the evening in January, the sky was pitch black. The downtown street lights glowed, with little auras of rainbow around each one, the result of the moisture in the high humidity Mississippi Valley. She went down the stone steps of the Rev. Reis's converted shelter. It had been some kind of city structure long ago, a courthouse or something that had fallen into disuse and the Reverend had bought it. Anna Lee had a vague memory of having been in it years ago, before her sickness.

    She walked at her usual pace, for fear the Reverend might be watching her out the front window, but inside she wanted to run so badly. She had told Jason to wait for her in a small, block-long park one street over, and she was anxious to get back to him. She didn't realize what a toll the incident with the kitty had taken on her, but that was what was in her mind as she began to pick up speed. A patrol car came around the corner, two uniforms whom she knew inside, the one riding shotgun opening the coffee. They waved at Anna Lee, who waved back and silently prayed they wouldn't spot Jason in the park. How in the world would she and the boy explain that? They kept going and she broke into a trot, practically leaping across the street to the park bench where he sat, away from a streetlight, in the shadows.

"Here ya go," she said, handing him the hat. "Now you won't have to wear my ol' scarf."

She smiled as he looked up at her and took it. He returned the smile; he felt safe with this crazy old black woman. She was big and she certainly wasn't pretty, although he wasn't so certain that she hadn't been in her youth. Her eyes were still very large, a little tip-tilted at the ends, black, and a strange combination of serenity and sadness looked out of them. Jason was only twelve years old and he didn't understand that he was looking into eyes that knew that resistance to the inevitable created a special kind of hell. These same eyes would glaze over with chemical imbalance and stare blindly, unknowing, at familiar places, faces and things. After it was over, they were always a little sadder.

"Thanks, Anna Lee. I 'preciate this," he said as he unwound the neck scarf from his head and put the hat on.

It was an old porkpie, a relic of another man's life in another time, and a little large for him. She had seen other hats that would have fit better, fisherman's caps and hats with earflaps, but somehow, she could visualize Jason in this little piece of silliness, and the thought appealed to her. It slid down to his eyebrows and he turned the brim up a little so he could see better. The streetlight lit up his young face as he looked up at her, the trust shining out of his eyes. The glow emphasized his own native beauty and, in spite of his clothing, he might have been something out of a Renaissance painting. There was also an effect similar to Lou Costello, the late comedian, who'd looked out at the world from under an upturned brim with the same innocence as this twelve-year-old boy.

Anna Lee looked at him, and started laughing. First it was quiet, and then, as she looked into his wondering eyes, it turned into large, rollicking guffaws, and she had to grab him and walk him swiftly up the sidewalk toward their alley. She needed to get him past Father Leon's place, so she had to stifle her laughter, but every time she looked down at the crown of the silly little hat, she would be overcome. Jason was smiling a little uncertainly, but her pleasure was infectious, and he began laughing, too, just because it was good to laugh, particularly with someone he trusted. Pretty soon, as they got abreast of Leon's mission, they were staggering with laughter, Anna Lee's hand over her mouth, making shushing gestures with the other one at Jason, while tears ran down her face.

They made it back to Anna Lee's grate in the alley, and collapsed on each other, laughing until they hurt, hugging each other, Anna Lee rocking Jason's slender body in her arms.

It was four a.m. Anna Lee and Jason were asleep; he closely cradled against Anna Lee's large, hospitable breast, poor old Willie the Wino with his back up against Anna Lee's. Frank O'Meara had taken a sleeping pill; the scotch was not working tonight, and he had lain too long, thinking about bloody urine, and was now sleeping fitfully, tossing in his bed.

Lorraine Anglethwaite was pacing her apartment floor, while Dodie slept on the couch. She wouldn't let her out of her sight; one child gone was enough. In fact, she wasn't even sure she that wouldn't keep Dodie home from school again in the morning.

Father Leon snored stuporously; he'd had a long day, two sick drunks, one had died on him. He hated that, when the Beast won. He knew everybody was going to die, but, oh, dear Lord, couldn't it be because the machinery had just worn out, not because something ugly had conquered?

And Sean Patrick O'Herlihy was strutting out to his car, feeling quite satisfied within himself, like he had just gotten laid. The trouble was that he had no actual memory of such an event. He could recall going to Rita's apartment, some conversation, but everything after that was a blank; he did have an unpleasant piece of memory that kept coming back to him, where he was holding her down on the floor, pressing her wrists into the carpet, and screaming into her face something about being a "fuckin' little whore," and "fuckin' little tease," and her crying and struggling. But that was all.

Sometimes this happened to him, he would suddenly come to in a place, and not know how he'd gotten there, or find himself in the middle of a conversation with someone he didn't know, and not know what he'd said two seconds before. He always managed to act like he knew exactly what was going on, and congratulated himself on fooling everybody. The baffled look in their eyes was proof that he was smarter than they. So he stopped worrying about it. He knew that this was just one of those things that happened to everybody, but nobody talked about, like going to the bathroom. He got into his car, started it up, threw it into gear, whistling all the while, and drove away. He'd have time to shower, shave, maybe grab a bite before roll call.

Frank got some sleep from the sleeping pill, but it wasn't good sleep, and he was awake about twenty minutes before his usual hour and his alarm clock. He shut the alarm down at his bedside before it could ring; actually, it didn't ring, but made an annoying series of buzzes that would go off at intervals, and he surely didn't want to hear it this morning.

He lay there, remembering fifteen years of conversation with Leon Devereux. As he thought about the years, the interminable chess game, the gallons of coffee, he realized what a deep fondness he had for the priest. He was too embarrassed to call it love, although it met all the criteria. He knew, as he thought about it, that if anyone asked him who his best friend was, he would unhesitatingly name Leon. He didn't know when or how this had come to pass, only that it had, and it brought tears of gratitude to his eyes. Over time, his admiration for the man had grown prodigiously. He had known very little about him, and, although a cradle Catholic, the priesthood was a thing of mystery to him.

He had never been particularly close to his brother, Kevin, whom he loved, but with whom he shared nothing. He couldn't understand Kevin's ability to turn his back on the unkindness of the world, and considered his vocation a cop-out. He hid in a rectory in an upscale neighborhood, dealing with the problems of the well-to-do, and Frank found this all extremely distasteful. He considered Kevin's dedication to God a sham.

On the other hand, as a cop who worked the streets, he was completely baffled by Leon's ability to get up every day, face the human wreckage that came his way, fight for every dime that kept the mission going, and still maintain his belief in God and His love. Early on, he had thought maybe Leon was a little tipped in the wrong direction, and one day, without saying exactly those words, indicated as much.

Leon had started laughing, a huge, mirthful explosion from this normally soft-spoken man and said, "I was wondering when you were going to say it, Frank. I've known all along that you think I'm a little crazy. Let me ask you: why do you do what you do? I mean, why are you a policeman? Why did you decide to become a clean-up man for the rest of the world? Did you think you could make a difference?"

"Well, yeah, I guess I did. I mean, I never really thought a lot about it. I just knew from the time I was a little kid that bein' a cop was what I wanted to do. My father was one, and it seemed natural enough that I would be one. And, I suppose that I started out with a certain amount of idealism. Although," he hastened to add, "I was already familiar with how bad it could be, from stories my dad brought home. And I knew that he wasn't tellin' the really bad stuff; he wasn't one to bring garbage home to his family just to be wallowing in it."

Leon said, "Well, even as a small child, Frank, I, too, knew that I had a thing to do." His eyes grew distant, looking over the chessboard, past Frank's shoulder, to another time in a faraway place. "You know, Frank, I come from quite a lot of money. My father was a planter in the Cameroons."

Frank did not know this, and was very startled to find out. Wealthy aristocracy in Africa had never occurred to him. He wasn't a bigot, as much as just narrow in his thinking. The first time Leon had spoken to him in perfect English with that rat-a-tat-tat accent had shocked him down to the soles of his feet, although he hoped that he had covered it well. In his experience, black men spoke a particular argot with a particular music, and to hear something else issuing out of this black mouth took him by surprise. It had been the first thing that had piqued his cop curiosity, and had caused him to return. Then he just kept coming back because Leon was, simply put, good to be around.

He sat up straight and paid attention. This

was the first time Leon had ever mentioned his background. Leon fiddled with the chess pieces, centering some that were close to the edges of their squares, slid down in his chair, then stretched his long legs and laced his fingers behind his head.

"Did it never occur to you to wonder why my name is 'Devereux'? In the Bantu tongues of my people, nobody is named 'Devereux'."

Actually, Frank had wondered, but assumed that some white French blood had gotten mixed in somewhere, not uncommon in some southern areas of the U.S. He knew nothing about Africa.

"My great-grandfather was a Frenchman. He left a wife and children in Paris, and came to the Cameroons to make his fortune in rubber. He certainly did that, and started a second line, also. He never married my great-grandmother, but he provided for her and their offspring handsomely. He saw to it that my grandfather and his siblings were well educated, both by European standards, and in ways that were suitable to their culture. My grandfather was trained to run the plantation after finishing school in France, and he increased the family fortune considerably. We Devereux have lived well ever since.

"I have an older sister, but I was my father's first son. I know when I chose the priesthood he was disappointed, but he covered it well, and was most supportive. Right now, if I wanted to, I could go back to the Cameroons and live like a king. My younger brother runs the family business in partnership with my sister's husband, they do well, and I know that a portion is kept in escrow for me. I don't have to stay here and do what I do. Now you know how crazy I really am," he smiled.

Frank looked at him. Leon had what Frank called "class." Leon was charming and gracious to a fault, only raised his voice when he could not be heard, and was unfailingly courteous. All this, Frank felt, was wasted on Leon's clientele, none of whom Frank believed was capable of being grateful for this remarkable man's hospitality. If any one of them was aware of how Leon struggled to keep his shelter going, Frank had not known them to say so.

"Well, are you going to tell me why, or should I just guess?" Frank said.

Leon chuckled softly. "I don't think I could ever explain to your satisfaction what my vocation means to me. You have a brother who is a priest, don't you, Frank?"

"Yeah, Kevin's pastoring a parish out in Chesterfield, St. Claire of Assisi, I believe."

"Well, have you never asked him why he entered the seminary?"

"No, I haven't. I just made certain assumptions, I guess, and, well, to tell the truth, we were raised in the Irish Catholic tradition, and it was just assumed that somebody would either become a nun or a priest. I don't remember exactly when it became obvious that Kevin was the lucky winner, and that I would be the cop; it was another one of those things that we just seemed to know."

Frank's eyes also had grown distant here, looking back down the years, past the barricade of time. He had known he would be a policeman, Kevin would be a priest, and that Teresa would have children. Nobody knew then that this was the last generation of this branch of the O'Mearas.

Frank had expected to have some children of his own, and he didn't like to think too often about the fact that he didn't. That unfilled niche in his life would gnaw at him sometimes, in these dark hours before dawn, when he laid there as he did now, alone, feeling like an aging failure. Where had the time gone? Why didn't he have a family of his own? These were questions he couldn't bear to ponder. And they were starting to eat at him now, as he thought about blood in his urine, and Leon's comment about the quantities of scotch he consumed. This was not the way it was supposed to end.

Chapter Five

***DAY TWO**, January 30th*   Sean sauntered out to the garage to join Phillips in the cruiser; it was seven-forty-five am, and roll call was over. He had fidgeted through it all, looking around to see if Rita had showed up. He didn't really care about seeing her, as much as he felt like strutting a little. She hadn't, and he just assumed that maybe today was her day off or she worked a different shift or whatever. How the hell would he know? He wasn't her keeper.

The concrete underground garage was cold, silent and empty as he looked around for the car he and Phillips usually took out. Ordinarily, after roll call, it was full of chattering uniforms, engines belching, car doors slamming. For a minute, he stood there puzzling, and then Ray Stillwater and his buddy, Stan Olsen, materialized out of the cold shadows. Stan stood quietly behind him, while Ray came up into his face. Ray was tall, topping six foot three, and Sean, at five foot eleven, had to look up at him.

"Hey, Stillwater, what's happenin'?" He didn't like Stillwater, didn't like his style, but he didn't have time to put him in his place right now, so he'd just be courteous and move on.

As he started to move around him, Ray

blocked him. Sean frowned, looking up at him. "Stay away from Rita, asshole," said Stillwater, looking down at him menacingly.

Sean tensed up. Stillwater was about ten years younger than he, and had a good thirty pounds on him. So Sean thought he'd play the old bull and try simple intimidation. Instead of responding to the statement, he attacked the behavior.

"Outta my way, Rookie. I gotta partner waitin' for me and a shift to work."

Stillwater stepped closer to Sean and said, "Your partner is enjoying an extra cuppa coffee this mornin', and I'm tellin' ya: keep away from Rita. She's off limits to you."

"What is it with you? Are you her boyfriend?" Sean was genuinely puzzled by this behavior that seemed to go beyond the friendships that were established in the Academy.

"I'm a married man, cocksucker, and I'm not trash like you. I don't cheat on my wife. But Rita is my friend. She's Stan's friend, too, and we look out for each other. You ever even so much as say her name again, and I'll feed you your own stones."

Sean was stunned. What was this guy's problem? "Look, man, I don't know what your beef is, but I got things to do. Now just back off, and nobody'll have any pain problems."

Once again, he moved to get around Stillwater, and once again, was cut off. He felt, more than saw, Olsen advancing toward his back. Stillwater grabbed the fake fur collar of Sean's navy blue winter jacket.

"You know damned well what my beef is, you cheap little motherfucker. Now, I don't care where you go, what you do, or who you do it with, but I'm tellin' ya, asshole, you're a disgrace to the Force, and the fact that Rita cares about the Force is all that's keepin' her from bringin' you up on charges. If I had my way, you'd be locked up for the rest of your useless life, and get the shit kicked outta ya three times a day. In fact, I just might do that anyway, just for fun."

For about three seconds, Sean's mouth hung open in amazement. Then he gathered up his cool. Couldn't let some rookie think he's got the upper hand here.

Very quietly he said, "Stillwater, take your hands off my collar and get outta my way."

To his surprise, Stillwater did just that. As he walked away towards his patrol car, he realized that he still didn't quite understand why Stillwater had such a hard-on for him. Then he just decided that, married or not, he and Rita had a thing going, and he was marking off his territory. Well, guess what, ha ha! A better man had been there (he thought).

He found the cruiser, unlocked the door, got in behind the wheel, and fired it up. Usually Phillips drove, but since he was havin' that extra cuppa joe Sean would get things started. Then the oddity of the entire morning began to hit him: the emptiness of the garage, Phillips' second coffee in the stationhouse. What the hell was goin' on here?

Well, Sean was not a man to worry overly much about the inexplicable, which was what most of his life had been to him. All he cared about was, well, whatever it was that he cared about, like gettin' that bitch of an ex-wife to ease up the screws on him, seein' his boy when he wanted, havin' a little fun once in a while, and enough money to do it on. Why the hell did everything have to be so fucked up? Every time he turned around, he was gettin' kicked in the balls, if not by his bitch of an ex-wife, then some rookie, some bullshitter, who didn't have near the cools that he, Sean Patrick O'Herlihy, had. Why did he have to put up with all these losers? He suddenly remembered a little bumper sticker he had seen years ago, when he was in his teens: "How can I soar like an eagle when I'm surrounded by turkeys?" Well, that was okay. He'd shake these turkeys, leave 'em all behind. He'd show 'em. Stupid little fuckin' losers didn't appreciate an all-around standup guy like himself.

His musings were interrupted when Phillips opened the door on the driver's side and told him to scoot over, which he did. Again he noticed something odd, this time in Phillips' behavior, although he couldn't pin it down. He thought it might be because, while Phillips ordinarily avoided eye contact with him (proof of what a jerk he was), this morning he seemed to give Sean a surreptitious once-over. Well, who gave a rat's ass? Not Sean Patrick O'Herlihy, that was for damned sure. Just another loser, a stupid fuckin' nigger, and wunna these days, he'd be rid of him, too.

Chapter Six

Frank O'Meara was also having a second cup of coffee, over which he was arguing with himself. He sat there on his living room couch, television blaring one of the morning shows to which he was oblivious. He was preoccupied with weighing the pros and cons of this physical that Leon had urged so strongly. Yes, he should go to the doctor. Outside of the annual physical given by the department doctor, he didn't have regular checkups. The annual department checkup was fairly cursory, given the time and number of cops to be looked over. Blood pressure, respiratory system, weight, and the canned lecture on diet and exercise, which was unchanged from year to year (he wondered if it was matched to his health needs which never seemed to change, or if the other cops got the same one) ended with the word, "next." Now, however, he knew that he needed an in-depth examination, with particular attention to the urinary problem.

There were several reasons why he hesitated. First of all, he hated time spent in the waiting room, waiting for the doctor in the examination room, and all the time waiting for the closing chat in the doctor's office. It all seemed a waste of time better spent doing something else. The second reason was that sometimes physicals are uncomfortable. He understood the feminine objection to a pap smear. But the third reason was the real reason: he just didn't want to know. If it was something terrible, it either meant protracted treatment, or no treatment at all, just a death sentence. And, frankly, he almost preferred the death sentence to the prospect of a long, complicated treatment, which may or may not work.

He rubbed the bridge of his nose, thinking about the options, none of which appealed. The least appealing, however, would be Leon's disappointment that he wasn't doing something. Leon believed that no situation was hopeless, unless a person did not act.

He set his cup and saucer on the small coffee table and likewise his feet onto it (his ex-wife would have had a fit), and, lacing his fingers behind his head, leaned back and thought about his friend, Leon. Eternally optimistic, Leon was convinced that underneath all the misery, the cosmos was exactly as it should be. Nothing, no event in human history that Frank could dredge up, could shake Leon's faith in the rightness of the Creator and His creation.

Most of their conversation, punctuated by

chess moves and lubricated by a river of coffee, had pivoted on the eternal question of the existence of evil. If there is a loving God Who is all good, whence all the bad stuff? If this God was not the author of it, then how could He permit it? If He was unable to stop it, then obviously He was not all-powerful. If He was able to stop it and didn't, then He was not as loving as His PR people would have you believe. What was it Leon told him Augustine had said? Ah, yes, "If God is benevolent then He is not omnipotent; if He is omnipotent then He is not benevolent." As Leon said, the great Jobian conundrum.

Frank just could not make sense out of a loving God on the one hand, and an event like the Jewish Holocaust on the other. Not to mention the numerous smaller disappointments of his own life. He had three choices: God doesn't care, exist, or have power. He didn't care which of the three he chose, because the net result was the same: no relief from the constant pounding of the pain.

One day he had come in from a homicide scene in which an unemployed man had held his wife and two small children hostage for several hours, barricaded in an old flat. It was a white family where the father had lost his job some months prior, and felt that the world in which he lived would never provide another. Neighbors and police gathered outside, trying to talk him out. A pastor from a small neighborhood church had come by to pray with him, if the man would allow. The upshot of it all was that the man killed his wife and children, then turned the weapon on himself.

Frank had been called in with the rest of the cleanup crew, three homicides and a suicide. After doing the necessary, he was heartsick. What he had seen, the two dead little children lying on their sides, their mother with half her face gone, he knew would stay with him for a long time. He could easily visualize the scene, the placement of the bodies told the whole story. As the man first turned the gun on the youngest child, the mother ran to the little boy, putting herself between the barrel of the weapon and the little one. The trigger would have been squeezed, and her head would have jerked back as she fell onto her back. Then, quickly, quickly, he would have shot the little boy, and then turned toward the girl, about seven years old, who would have run to her mother's body. Kneeling beside her mother's corpse, she would have been looking up at him in horror as he once again squeezed on the trigger. She fell onto her side, across her mother's body, one arm protectively over the woman's belly. Finally, in a last convulsion of pain, he would have jammed the barrel into his mouth and found the anesthetic he so badly craved. They would join the legion of faces that paraded by him in the nights when he couldn't sleep.

He came into the mission, and plopped himself on the old couch in Leon's office. Leon had looked up, nodded and smiled, and then returned to the bookkeeping he was doing. When he completed the task he swiveled around in his chair with his usual wide smile to greet his friend. The smile froze and then vanished as the expression on Frank's face was processed in Leon's brain.

"My God, Frank, you look like you've seen a ghost. What in the world is wrong?" Leon asked, concern clearly delineated all over him.

Frank twirled his little snap-brim hat on his finger, one foot propped on the scarred coffee table, and refused to meet Leon's eyes. He didn't want Leon to see the tears there, ready to spill over. If he didn't keep control, they would turn into a humiliating deluge.

Without raising his eyes, he said, "I just came from a homicide-cum-suicide; this guy shot his wife and kids, and then himself. He was jobless and hopeless, and now he's dead, and so's his family."

He was angry and hoping that Leon would

try to comfort him so he could lash out at him and his beliefs. It would feel good to curse the God who let all this happen. Silently, he dared Leon to offer some inane platitude about acceptance, taking the good with the bad, some such bullshit that was supposed to explain away the pain, the pain that Frank dealt with every day. Why should he, why should anybody, have to sort out such chaos? It was indefensible.

For a moment, Leon said nothing. He knew that triviality was the last thing that Frank needed now.

Softly, he said, "I'm so sorry, Frank. So very sorry that this happened."

Finally raising his eyes, Frank glared at him. "Are you really? Sittin' here, all cozy and nice in your little hidey-hole. You don't participate, you just try to make everybody else do it. You clean up a drunk, stand him up and send him out for more combat, more of the same. While you stay in here, all safe and sound, man, you're just like Kevin, all you priests and clergy. That idiot who came by to pray this afternoon, didn't he know that man didn't need prayer? He needed a job, he needed hope, NOT a bunch of pious bullshit from people who have no idea what it's like to really hurt."

He flung his hat across the room, crossed his arms and stared at the toe of his shoe on the coffee table.

Leon correctly surmised that Frank welcomed a good fight here, for a couple of reasons. One was to vent his anger, but more desperately, he needed to be reassured that he was not just shoveling sand against the tide.

In Frank's line of work, just as in Leon's, weariness turned easily to burnout. Leon knew that the underlying despair of burnout is the feeling of failure, uselessness, time wasted. Effort expended must bear some fruit, even if it is only the knowledge that the wrong soil was chosen for sowing. The belief that there is no acceptable soil, that all effort goes for naught, is a dangerous and frightening premise.

Leon understood what very few people do understand: that the same little mental doorway that admits pain is also the entrance for joy. One cannot be shut out without excluding the other. He knew that Frank needed to know that if he kept his little door open there would be the occasional intrusion of happiness.

"So what is it that you want from me, Frank? Some statement to the effect that life sucks and then you die? You certainly don't want comfort. What you do want is relief, and that I cannot give. If I agree with your nihilistic philosophy, I betray what I do truly believe, and, more importantly, I corroborate your worst fear.

Yet, if I offer some aphorism, you will dismiss it as a platitude and a copout, given by one who has no idea what 'real life' is like. Correct? So. How can I win with you? What do you want?"

Frank nodded. He had the grace to look ashamed; he knew he was being impossible, like a tired child in a tantrum. Actually, he was having an adult version of a tantrum, brought on by fatigue and frustration. It was not physical fatigue, but a psychic tiredness, a soul that was running on empty and had no hope of a refill.

"First of all, Frank, you should know that I am acquainted with pain. You think I am like your brother, Kevin, that all priests have simply retired from life, and we are spectators, not participants. Because we have not chosen the arena of a personal life, we are noncombatants.

"Well, let me tell you something, Frank, I don't know Kevin, and he may be every bit as cowardly as you say, but I am one of a host of people who have put aside the gratification of life in the world for another kind of combat. And I tell you, it is just as overwhelming as the war in which you engage."

"Oh, okay. Now comes the big speech about your sainted abstinence, how holy and pure you are 'cause you don't get laid. Wahoo! Boy, have I heard that one before. Kevin thinks he's entitled to a new Lincoln every year from his parishioners, just because he's celibate. Piss on your purity and your martyrdom. I don't get laid, either. It's just that I wouldn't pass up the opportunity if it came along. You, however, St. Leon, would roll your eyes heavenward and pray to St. Augustine to preserve you from temptation, and then walk manfully away from a nice, available piece of ass."

Leon threw back his head and laughed, white teeth flashing in the dim light against his dark chiseled face. "Ah, yes, Frank, ah, yes, I am the soul of purity, free of lust and impure thoughts. I have never kept a secret jar of petroleum jelly in my bedroom in my youth, nor did I ever have the pleasure of watching a shapely woman in tight pants walk away from me, and wish that I could do something about it."

He leaned forward, his arms resting on his thighs, heels of his hands together. "Frank, did you know that the Cameroons is full of some of the most beautiful women in the world? Dark, long-legged women with eyes you could drown in."

He leaned back, stretching his long legs in front of him, and laced his fingers behind his head. He looked at Frank from under lowered eyelids. "Frank, you know that I come from wealth; you know that I am an educated man, a qualified physician. You also know that I am not a homosexual. I am a healthy middle-aged man, with the same drives and desires you have, and I could easily satisfy them. I could go out into the world, armed as I am, and select a tasty dish from a smorgasbord of beautiful women. I could make a lot of money as a doctor; belong to the upper crust of black America. There are mothers out there who would kill in order to marry me to their daughters.

"Therefore, you conclude that since I don't take advantage of any of this, I am in hiding. You think that because I don't take the journey your way, I'm not taking it at all. I will concede that marriage is a very effective way of exploring the self. In order to be successful in such an intimate and volatile relationship, continuous honest self-appraisal is necessary. But it is not the only way.

"I challenge you, Frank. I submit that you are the one who's hiding," he did not mention at this point that he suspected Frank's attachment to the scotch bottle. "I tell you, it is easy to despair. It takes work and it takes honesty to hope. It takes a high level of energy, both physical and psychological, to not give in to the darkness. It is much easier to say, as your English character, Scrooge, 'Bah! Humbug!' to all that is good. It is easy to dismiss beauty as the illusion and treat evil as the only reality. That way you can live defensively, barricaded behind your despair, and never take chances because there are no chances to take."

Frank looked at him, and then got up and went across the room to retrieve his hat. He sat down again, elbows on knees, and put his head into his hands.

After wiping his hands down his face, he said, "I know that I'm being unfair, Leon, and I apologize. I just felt like being nasty for a minute, and I shouldn't have vented on you. But, I gotta tell you, sometimes I do wonder what you're hiding from. I'm a cop, and you are one of the most improbable people I've ever met. I could see a man with your background as a kid, gettin' all romantic about the priesthood, but I can't imagine somebody like you stickin' with it.

"And Kevin is hiding, and since he's the only priest I know really well, I guess I base my judgment about all priests on him. I know that one person does not a population make, so what Kevin does is probably irrelevant. But you gotta admit, lookin' at you, it's not unreasonable to think that you either got somethin' else goin' on, somethin' that you're not talkin' about, or that you're just not interested in livin' a life."

"Of course, you are quite right, Frank, and it is true that a good many people do try to use the clerical vows as a way of avoiding life. And the Church is desperate for people with vocations; the convents and the seminaries are being boarded up and sold off. However, we still have some pretty fair screening techniques; a lot of people who are trying to hide are discovered early on in the process, and never take final vows.

"I don't think, though, that you came here to discuss what makes a good candidate for Holy Orders." He waited expectantly.

Chapter Seven

Frank sighed. "Yeah, Lee, you're right." He got up and started pacing around the small office, running his fingers through his hair, trying to get his thoughts together. "I think that at some level, I envy you. I mean, look at us, you and me: we're both, in our own ways, garbage men. We clean up society's throwaways. You try to recycle it, I just try get it out of the way, and neither one of us ever succeeds."

He looked out the little window of the office that looked onto a view of the alley. Several dumpsters, overflowing, rusty and dented, were lined up. These were some of the places where the homeless foraged. There was a coffee shop close by, and several of the small businesses in the area also used them. Leftovers from people's lunches could be found occasionally here, stale merchandise from the vending machines, that kind of thing.

"In fact, between the two of us, you probably have the most discouraging job. You nurse some drunk through his DT's, clean 'im up, dress 'im up, feed 'im good, and six months later, he's back here.

"I pick up garbage and put it into the trash bin. Then some damned judge lets the garbage out, and I'm out there, pickin' up the same trash, over and over again, always gettin' there after some terrible damage has been done. I pick up the same trash, and then clean up his mess, and I see the horrible shit he does, and I just want to bury my fist in his face, until it feels spongy."

He slapped his right fist into his left palm, demonstrating his desire to punish. "But you, you never think, 'omagod, here we go again'. You just smile and say, 'Welcome back, we'll set a place for you', and the s.o.b. goes through the same routine again. You smile and bless 'im, you never get mad, and," here he paused in his pacing and looked at Leon, "you never think it's for nothing. How do you do that?"

Frank's naked frustration in that last question was almost comical, and Leon wanted to laugh, but caught himself. Still stretched out in the swivel chair, hands behind his head, he puffed his cheeks and slowly blew the air out of his lungs. How in the world could faith be explained to the faithless? How could trust be taught to the chronically disappointed?

Softly, almost in a whisper, he said, "Frank, I know despair. I know loneliness, and they have nothing to do with my priesthood. They are natural concomitants of my humanity. The fact is I am no different than you. I am susceptible to the same diseases of the soul that beset other men.

"Let me tell you something. There was a time when I lost sight of who I am, forgot why I was born, and it took me down, Frank, it took me down. I didn't just have doubts; I was suicidal. I didn't understand what had happened, nor why. And that, sir, for your information, was the only time in my life I ever invoked St. Augustine. I was having what he called a 'dark night of the soul'." This last was said with a rueful smile, redolent of painful memories.

The surprise on Frank's face, along with the slow "I knew it" look spoke volumes. Frank hadn't been kidding when he'd said that Leon baffled him. Their friendship was still young when this conversation took place. Frank had never known Leon except as a compassionate priest, a man absolutely dedicated to the disadvantaged. He kept doing the same thing, over and over, day in and day out, and never seemed daunted by it. The occasional flash of anger from frustration by the bureaucracy was the closest to negative Frank had ever seen in Leon's behavior. Otherwise, he had a serenity that Frank envied wholeheartedly. Periodically, he would join Leon to celebrate Mass in the early morning. Then he could see the absolute commitment that Leon felt to this God, whom he clearly adored. Frank knew in his heart that Leon was not a hypocrite, but damned if he could explain him.

"I always knew I was destined for the priesthood, since I was a small boy in the Catholic school in the village close to our home. There was a priest and two sisters who taught us there."

His eyes no longer saw Frank, but a distant time and place. A sweet memory was replaying itself in Leon's head. He came back to the present and looked at Frank.

"Our father insisted that we take the best of our European heritage, and surely, for us, the Church was a part of that." He stood up, picked up his coffee cup and raised his eyebrows at Frank.

"Yeah, sure, Lee, I'd like a refill." Frank was curious now, waiting. He knew, good cop that he was, that he was about to hear a confession. He'd play along.

Leon returned with the coffee, steam snaking out of the cups. He handed Frank's to him, and set his own down on the desk. He sat down again in the swivel chair and examined his hands, front and back. Frank waited quietly.

"I was a fortunate child, Frank, and an equally blessed young man. As you have probably already surmised, I wanted for nothing. I was not pampered, but I was much loved.

"When I was old enough, I went to school

in France. I think that my father hoped that the time there would cause me to reconsider my lifelong desire to be a priest, and that I would return to help him with the plantation. He was right insofar as I did my share of partying. I was young, healthy, I came of good family, family with money, and many young women were interested in becoming a part of that family.

"You see, Frank, in France persons of African extraction are considered very attractive people. Not like here in the United States, where I am regarded as some kind of freak. 'Oh, look here, a black man who is literate.' A lot of white Americans consider persons of color to be some kind of superior talking ape. And if Caucasians become romantically involved with them, it is for amusement, not for real." He said this latter with some bitterness.

Frank had never seen this side of Leon, and he was absolutely still. Leon was constitutionally unable to sustain an angry or vindictive emotion for any period longer than ten seconds. So as Frank watched, the playful young boy Leon had been took over and laughed out at him from behind the adult priest's face.

"You see, Frank, what you don't understand is that I made informed choices. So, I had a good time in Paris, and when I finally went into the seminary, I will admit I was no longer a virgin. I say this without shame, guilt or regret. It's just the way it is.

"You know, Frank," he said, while closely examining his hands, "not all cultures have the sexual self-consciousness that you Americans have.

"Anyway, I think my father had counted on my natural drives to turn me around, make me want to remain in the world. Actually, all it did was confirm what I already knew." Here he ceased the intense study of his hands, and looked directly at Frank. "Do not misunderstand. I enjoyed all my experiences. In fact, it was a veritable Arabic garden of delights." He leaned back again, hands behind his head, and looked at the ceiling, smiling. "Ha, yes, beautiful women, all sizes, shapes and colors. Sometimes, at night, I can still taste them, smell them, feel their silky hides under my hands." Again he looked directly at Frank, quiet pleasure in his eyes. "And I am grateful for these memories. But all that only served to underscore what I already knew: sweet as they were, I still heard a voice infinitely sweeter. Try as I might, the hunger I had could only be fed by my vocation. And so, that's what I did."

He sighed. "This is simply inexplicable to anyone who hasn't experienced it. I know. Those of us who have are even sometimes a little dubious about it. During my seminary years, there was much debate about the properties of a 'true vocation', as we young seminarians called it. It always finally came down to what your Louie Armstrong once said about jazz."

Both Leon and Frank were jazz lovers, another pleasure they shared, and were familiar with the legend of Louie Armstrong, who was reputed to having answered, when asked to define jazz, "Man, if you got to ask, you ain't never gonna know."

Leon continued. "I knew that there was nothing that would satisfy me except a complete dedication of my life to God. Does this mean that I didn't sometimes long for the things of the world? Of course not! I thought about perhaps affiliating myself with the Church in some way that would allow me to marry, have a woman, children, but I knew that would be so unfair to any family I had. It would be cheating both them and God. My passion for God was so strong, it would suffer no parceling out of my energies, my focus. Crazy, huh? But there are others like me in this world, Frank. We are as we are, and there is simply no compromise.

"So. There I was, all full of my vocation. My father's disappointment could not stop me, and to be fair, he was very decent about it. Until he died, though, I know that he secretly entertained the hope that one day I'd grow tired of what he considered silly self-deprivation, and come home to carry on his project, the plantation that he loved. He couldn't see the priesthood as a project, just some ridiculous hobby for people who can't make it otherwise. And he was an active Catholic. It was years before I understood that my father, in his heart, had a very private relationship with God that had nothing to do with the Church.

"Anyway, I took Holy Orders, and since I had always had a bent for biology, it seemed natural enough that the Church would use that, and I took up medicine.

"Oh, I tell you, Frank, I am well trained. I studied at the Sorbonne in France, in Austria, and finally, here, in the United States. I was interested in several areas. I thought about specializing in psychiatry, and also I was intrigued by liver functions, but I finally settled on diseases of the blood, malaria, sickle cell anemia, leukemia, and the like. I was fascinated by the ability of the body's blood cells to manufacture defenses, and wanted to know why sometimes it would fail. And I was good, Frank, very good at what I did, a scientist of some substance. I studied, I researched and I made some contributions, enough to get the attention of the St. Louis University Hospital and School of

Medicine. I was a natural for it. Not only was I a Jesuit, but this was the sixties, when your countrymen were being forced to rethink their attitudes about persons of color. What better way of demonstrating good faith than by pushing a promising young African along in the hierarchy here? So I was brought here by Holy Mother Church and got the surprise of my life."

Here Leon paused and looked up at Frank. "Frank, do you know the word, 'naif'?" Frank shook his head. "Well," he continued, "it's the noun form of a French word that has been considerably anglicized, 'naive'. And that's what I was, a genuine naif. Oh, of course, all over the world, we knew about your racial problems, your riots, the unhappiness concerning Vietnam. The rest of the world looked on with some amusement.

"You have no idea what a barrier the Atlantic Ocean is. It really hinders America's global relationships. I, as a person raised under the vestiges of French colonialism, could certainly appreciate the Vietnamese need for national identity. As a person of color, I simply laughed at the ridiculousness of the anti-black bigotry.

"I assure you, Frank, the U.S. does not have a monopoly on bigotry. In Canada, it is the French-Canadians who are considered unworthy.

In France, it is the Arabs, and all over the world, Jews are mistrusted. The Irish are the 'niggers' of northwestern Europe, so I am very familiar with the effects of prejudice. I had always felt I was above it, and, because I was never in a place to get a good dose of it, I never knew how it felt.

"Until I came here. When it began to dawn on me what a strange and incongruous thing I was in the eyes of my fellow doctors, most of whom were Caucasians of good family, I can't tell you how this affected me. In those days, there were not so many Asians in American medical schools. We of different appearance were not common, and I was the only black doctor on the staff. My foreignness was tolerable, but my blackness, no matter how hard they tried, was not acceptable. To the credit of my fellows, they tried, they really tried. But the gulf between us was truly vast. And I, for my part, was having a bad time concealing my contempt for their provinciality. As an antidote for severe loneliness, I threw myself into my research. I did well, too, but I was so competitive that I completely alienated everybody. I did well in my studies, very well, and I would lord it over the others. Then I could console myself by the thought that they were jealous of my success. I did not know what to do, I was in such pain."

For a moment he was silent, and the memory of suffering showed on his face. "I had never in my life been 'weighed in the balance and found wanting', as Holy Scripture says. This was an entirely new experience for me, and no matter what I had read or heard on the news when I was in Europe, I was never prepared for the full effect of what mindless bigotry can do. It's like a slow drip of acid on the psyche, Frank. No matter how hard you try, sooner or later, it eats through the fiber, and you begin to believe what others insist that you are. My identity was slipping away, and I had no way of reinforcing it. The only feedback I got ran the spectrum from neutral to negative. The only time I felt good about myself was in my research, but I could share my triumphs with no one. I was caught in a negative cycle; all the blacks I knew despised me for betraying their cause. They were, after all, American, and felt that my blackness was sufficient reason for me to involve myself in their civil rights movement. I didn't feel that way at all. I was not a black American, but a man who was born and raised in Africa, and my skin color was black, not my soul. My soul was African and proud, too proud for its own good. While I thought it commendable, I could not identify at all with their cause.

"And my white colleagues had no use for

me - I was black, and there was no getting around that. Worse, I was very different from their experience of what a black man should be, and this caused them enormous discomfort. I was a constant burr under their collective saddle, not only by what I was, but by my attitude. I was really quite uppity. My research was good, which was offensive to white boys for whom a black man with an intellect was the source of much confusion. Nor would I assume the meek attitudes they expected from those they considered their inferiors.

"In fact, I was getting out and out belligerent. More than once I got into real shoving matches. All I had was my scholarship and I would not stand for it to be challenged. On the one or two occasions when my adversary was right and I was wrong, I would break things; once it was a young intern's nose. I was counseled for these outbursts, but everyone was being so careful of both my blackness and my very good research. My God, I was lonely. The Asians, while nice to me, clung together, and I had no place in their little clique. I was lonely and angry, and each fed the other. I could have gone to my superiors and asked to go home, but that would have been an admission of failure, that the white boys had won.

"And I certainly did not want my parents

to know what was happening to me. My dear mother, whom I adored, would have been inconsolable, and my father's blood pressure would have been elevated to lethal heights. No, my unhappiness was my own, and I would take care of it."

He paused to sip his coffee and quietly reminisce. Looking again at Frank, he said, "And take care of it I most certainly did. There was a young nurse at the hospital, just lovely. I remember looking at her blond hair, and thinking I had never seen that shade of blond outside of Scandinavia. I once spent a summer there. Handsome folk, the Nordics, and wonderfully hospitable.

"Anyway, one day she came into my lab. We were acquainted, but not especially friendly, and I really don't think that, outside of noticing that she was very pretty, I gave a second thought to her. We would smile, speak in passing, and that was all. I had never worked with her. So, she came into the lab where I was working, and I happened to notice a large bruise on her arm, I mean, really bad looking. She saw me look at it, and was embarrassed. She tried to adjust her sleeve to cover it. It was summertime here, in your hot St. Louis, and everyone was wearing short sleeves. She made some feeble joke about her clumsiness, but the wind was up with me. I knew there was something else here, and I meant to find out what it was." He grinned at Frank. "Sometimes I'm like you. I smell something and I just have to ferret it out, or I cannot rest. Maybe I should have been a priest-cop, huh?

"Anyway, I pursued the issue and found out that she was married to a mean drunk. She was what is called in current parlance an ACA, a codependent and a battered woman." He looked at Frank expectantly. "You know ACA?"

Frank shook his head. Damn! Another expression Leon knew and he didn't. Cops were supposed to be hipper than civilians and this so was embarrassing.

"ACA stands for Adult Child of an Alcoholic. This syndrome has been correctly identified in the last twenty years or so by people in the mental health field. I won't go into all the symptoms, but suffice it to say, when you understand the psychology of it you appreciate the fact that bruises like hers are an inevitability. I, of course, knew nothing of this, only that I was appalled. My father would have cut his hands off before raising them to my mother. As a matter of fact, wife beating is considered, where I come from, a cause for great shame for a man, never to be bragged about, and seldom happens.

"Somehow, I don't recall how or when, she began confiding in me. And I had a target for my free-floating rage. I had fantasies about what I would like to do to the subhuman who was brutalizing this lovely creature. I would be her hero, I would rescue her from this situation.

"Somewhere in all that mess, we became lovers. I forgot my vows, she no longer felt bound by hers. We couldn't keep our hands off each other, we'd rendezvous in the lab, the linen closet, empty hospital rooms, whatever. I was obsessed with her, and my work began to suffer. I felt that I deserved some relief from the pain which had been dogging me, and frankly speaking, my friend, my depression had reached such proportions that the very fact that I could get an erection again seemed a sign from God that this was a good thing for me to do. Most of all, it kept me from looking at what was happening to me. I could focus on this affair, keeping it both going and secret occupied my every waking moment, and nothing else mattered. I was running in place, trying to get away from the pain.

"I don't know how long this would have gone on, or what I would have eventually done. I told her to leave her husband, and we'd return to the Cameroons, we'd get married, we could leave all this misery behind. Of course, the very idea! This poor girl had been running on empty since she was a child; she had no idea what she wanted, she was a caretaker with no identity. The only time she felt like she was actively loving was when she was in pain. And I, of course, was completely divorced from reality. We were simply feeding each other's unreality, if there is such a word. I don't want to say fantasy, because this was really sick. There is no beautiful aura around it of, say, Walt Disney magic. We were really crazy, and we both knew that eventually confrontation with the truth was unavoidable. Nevertheless, we kept obsessively meeting.

"Oh, boy, Frank, I was some stallion; also an acrobat." He laughed a little shamefaced. "You'd be amazed at the things you can do in a supply closet if you're limber enough. And, of course, the element of risk considerably heightened the excitement. I think I became addicted to my own adrenaline. I know we were both using the sex and the excitement to change our realities." He looked sideways at Frank. "Much as policemen learn to like living on the edge, until they can't live normally anymore, that's how we were.

"Then, one day I was in my lab at the hospital, just piddling around. I was long past anything useful. I was simply marking time until I saw Sharon again - that was the young lady's name. I heard the door open and imagine my surprise, when I turned around to face my confessor.

"Now, Frank, you have to understand that I had been avoiding him for some time. He was both white and rather unimaginative, and I couldn't bring myself to confide in him. Worse than that, I felt that God had deserted me, left me to wander about in this racist wilderness, without hope, without purpose. Why should I go talk to this old man who would be appalled, recommend things like self-flagellation and large doses of saltpeter, all night prayer vigils kneeling on gravel, and other medieval lunacy. Nobody knew what they were talking about, least of all he. To me, he was just a bloodless old man, much as you perceive me."

Frank opened his mouth, but Leon brushed his protests aside with a wave of his hand. "Now, be honest, Frank; admit that you have doubts sometimes about my humanness, my manhood. But, anyway, while I made no pretensions to special knowledge of my own, I knew that I had no wish to continue to be a dupe. I felt that all the promises, implicit and explicit, had been at best misrepresentations of reality. I could not go home and admit defeat, nor could I stay here and suffer defeat. And there was nowhere else for me to go.

"This moment of confrontation with my

confessor was the beginning of the nadir of my life. I never saw Sharon again. I heard that she'd been fired. I never knew. I wanted to call her, but I was afraid that any call from me would precipitate another bout of violence from her husband. The other nurses would not speak to me; it was useless to ask them to check on her for me. The scandal was all over the hospital, despite the administration's efforts to keep it quiet. A black savage had been screwing a lily-white blond. Oh, my God! Here was the nightmare of King Kong, come true. A brute in priest's clothing, and a complete disgrace to the Church."

He grinned mischievously. "Actually, I felt more like Othello, but that failed to impress my superiors. The disciplinary committee told me that my violation of the vow of chastity was the reason I was being sent away; not a word was said about the real reason. I'd hate to tell you how many of my brother priests were engaged in discreet liaisons with women, and sometimes with other men, some of them priests also. No, sex was not the reason. Blondness and blackness was. Within forty-eight hours I was packed off to a rest home for alcoholic priests in Arizona. I had been instructed, really warned, to consider carefully my vocation, how badly I wanted it, if at all, and how much longer I could keep my visa. The last thing I wanted was for the disgrace to touch my family. I spent several months in Arizona, trying to sort out my mind. I prayed a lot, but most of the time, I was pretty sure I was talking to the void." He paused, and looked at Frank.

Frank said nothing, but there was a look of "Amen, brother" in his eyes. It was the look of a man who had been there and felt the feelings. If Frank understood anything at all, he understood loneliness and despair.

Leon continued. "After a month or so there, I started getting bored, so I went out to one of the reservations." He looked at Frank, an old compassion still very much alive in his eyes. "Frank, you just have no idea what is going on with your Native Americans, the alcoholism, the breakdown of family relations, the unemployment. This same thing happened in the Congo when the British came in during the nineteenth century.

"There is a book about the breakup of Obi culture; it is called *Things Fall Apart.* I recommend it for people who don't understand what happens when a cultural system is undermined.

"But, anyway, sociological treatises aside, I began going out there. I encountered a certain amount of prejudice there also, some aimed at my color, but most of it at my religion. The American Indian truly despises the Catholic Church, and that is the fault of Mother Church herself. But I managed to win a couple of friends over, and I began working at a Native American center, taking care of the drunks who came in, trying to treat diseases of the liver, most of them fatal. As I said earlier, liver diseases were one of my original interests, until I discovered that wonderful substance called blood. Anyway, usually when a drunk gets to the point that he's aware of liver damage, it's too late. But I knew how to make them comfortable, I could ease the pain, I had access to drugs that helped a little bit. With true cirrhosis, Frank, it is not uncommon for the victim to be both blind and deaf, and sometimes paralyzed. The liver has ceased to neutralize the toxins that are a normal part of everyday living, and all kinds of peculiar things begin to happen to the brain. And the pain is constant. Even when they couldn't tell me about it, I knew it was there.

"Their pain began to distract me from my own. I no longer thought about it sixteen hours a day, now it was down to maybe eight." He laughed at his little joke. "So I began to do real medical work, not in a lab, but actually treating sick people who were in desperate need. I had never in my life seen truly desperate need, Frank.

This was my first experience with it. You know how you, as a cop, see the worst, all day, every day? The only time anybody ever calls you is when there is trouble. Well, all of a sudden, I was in that position, both as a priest and as a doctor. My presence became necessary at a deathbed or a sickbed. I would get a call, and automatically pack both my medical bag and the ointments of the last rites. I would go anywhere I was called, any hour of the day or night.

"I was completely unprepared for the things I saw. You know, one day I was in town, this small desert town, where nothing goes on from year to year, there is not even a movie house, but there are at least fifteen taverns. Anyway, I was walking on my way to pick up a few things at the drugstore, and as I was approaching one of the bars, some man came rushing out at top speed. Directly in front of the doorway, on the curb, stood a mailbox. This fellow went racing for it, opened the lid, thrust his head in as far as it would go, and dumped the contents of his stomach onto the United States mail. Then, at the same rate of speed, he turned right around and dashed back into the bar again. I tell you, Frank, I was so dumbfounded, I could not believe what I had just seen. There was a sort of black comedy about the whole thing, it looked like a cartoon, the way it seemed that his feet never stopped moving. It was like, you know Wiley Coyote? You know how his feet keep moving in the air? This was the same effect. At any rate, about a week later, that mailbox was gone; there were only four depressions in the concrete of the sidewalk where it had been. I don't like to imagine the poor mailman whose duty it was to pick up out of that box every day. It was after seeing a few more of the absurdities that intoxication from alcohol generates, along with some real tragedy, that I began to realize that I had a genuine opportunity here for something, comfort, healing, whatever."

Leon paused in his reflections, sipping on his coffee. He frowned into the cup, the contents of which had cooled off. "How about some fresh coffee?" He looked inquiringly at Frank.

At this point, Frank would have said "yes" to a live grenade, he was so hypnotized by Leon's tale. Leon picked up both cups, and Frank twirled his hat on his finger. Now, finally, he was getting some insight to this mysterious priest. He also knew that Leon would have laughed him right into the next county if he knew that Frank had considered him mysterious. With this tale that Leon was telling here, he was beginning to understand that actually Leon was not a secret, nor a puzzle. He was seeing that it was his own cynicism that had turned Leon into an unbelievable character. Frank, for a very long time, had been unable to accept Leon at face value. He was constantly searching for chinks in this man's extraordinary joi de vivre in the life that he had chosen. Frank just knew there had to be something. If this guy was for real, Frank would really like to have for himself some of what Leon had.

When Leon returned he set the cups down, and stretched. Sitting down again, he looked at Frank and said, "So, to continue." Frank's cop nature could never let this story go now. "Okay, so anyway, where was I? Ah, yes, I was finding out what it means to be a real doctor, not some scientist playing with theory in a lab.

"You know, Frank, the difference between applied life and just spectatorship? Of course you do. You accused me of it a while ago, and you're sure that's what your brother does. Well, it was on the reservation that I learned the difference. I was where the rubber hits the road, Frank; I was actually doing something meaningful. It took me a while to realize that something very different was happening to me. It didn't hit me all at once, but in small doses. And it was there that I actually found the Master Whom I serve, Whom I had thought I was serving.

"Frank, I know that you would dispute

this, but your work is a blessed endeavor. I tell you, Frank, you bring comfort, help and relief where you go. You may not always know it, and I'm sure you rarely feel adequate, but your very presence at tragic events brings strength to the players. I know, I've seen it. People rely on the policeman in much the same way that they do on the priest. The big difference is that I'm expected to make sense out of the tragedy for them, and you are supposed to contain it. We don't always meet those expectations, do we?"

At this Frank shifted his position on the couch, recrossing his right ankle over his left knee. He wasn't just feeling inadequate this day, but downright powerless. He would see those faces in the dark for many nights to come. "Yeah, but Leon, you aren't gettin' it. Why would a loving and involved God allow these choices to be made? Why wouldn't he protect the victims? Does He care or not? Can He help or not?"

Leon shifted in his chair and smiled gently at Frank. "It angers you that the job you do is necessary. What kind of God permits the circumstances to exist that forge criminals and monsters? First of all, Frank, God did not invent evil. Most of what you and your colleagues call evil is born of fear, pain and misunderstanding. The thing that is scariest to you as a cop is the one thing that frightens everybody: unpredictability. And unpredictability is the root of fear, pain and confusion. True evil is the result of choices, and defined by intent, and it is not random, but very purposeful. It is willfully choosing an act, with a conscious and informed indifference to its destructive effect on others, the only benefit of which is self-gratification for the actor. Giving in to the impulses; you always have a choice, Frank, and that is where evil comes from. The Jews call it the 'evil inclination.' These are carnal needs run amok. It is not evil to satisfy hunger; it *is* evil to steal food from someone who has just enough to satisfy his own and who is unable to defend himself. It is not evil to want sex; it is the height of evil to have sex with an unwilling and defenseless partner. It is not evil to feel anger; it is very evil to succumb to it. And, Frank, when I examine it, it always seems to me that it all comes down to one thing: the love of power. St. Paul said that the love is money is the root of all evil; I disagree. It is the love of power that is the root of all evil, although I will credit him insofar as money is a form of power. Love of power always results in the abuse of it, and by power, I mean the ability to make someone else do your will, whether they want to or not. When people talk about power that is generally what they mean, to do a thing just because you can. They never mean power over the self, self-control. The carnal urges that you have are God-given, so they cannot be evil. The choice to misuse them, which is strictly up to the individual, is. God should not take the rap for that. That's what He has us for, you are the Equalizer, I am the Explainer."

"Yeah, but Leon, you **STILL** aren't gettin' it. Why would a loving and involved God allow these choices to be made? Why wouldn't he protect the victims? I repeat: does He care or not? Can He help or not? So much of the time, you don't even get a warning."

"Ah, Frank, everybody wants to see around the corners, or better yet, have no corner at all, but a straight road to the horizon, without interference from the right or the left. You think that those people in Kevin's parish have that straight road, no concerns at all, while others have to shift for themselves, and, as you Irish say, the divil take the hindmost. Too bad for them, it's just the luck of the draw. In the meantime, God sits somewhere in some celestial paradise and coolly observes our struggles.

"Frank, theology has never been my long suit, and I know that you consider me a hopeless innocent, somebody who lives in denial of the so-called 'reality.' You know, Frank, the noun 'reality' does not always have to be modified by the adjective, 'grim.' And innocence is not synonymous with ignorance, but is actually a balanced view of the world. The true innocent manages to gaze into Nietzsche's abyss, and when the abyss gazes back, it's the abyss that blinks, not the innocent. As strange as it may seem, I know that this universe is balanced. It's hard to see; faith and hope are like two candles in a hurricane. How can these two little flames withstand the great battering wind that we call life? It seems such a one-sided battle, you blow on those two little flames until you're panting to keep them alive, and then you have to keep your cupped hands around them because they are so fragile. And yet, when properly tended, they are more than enough to keep back the dark and the chaos. You see, Frank, that thing which you dread so, the unpredictable event, isn't always bad. Keep your little candles going, and at some point, the darkness will recede, and life will become a gentle breeze for a while. You know as well as I that the only constant in life is its inconstancy. The biggest challenge any human being faces is to live in the Now, where sometimes it's uncomfortable, maybe even dangerous. And yet the Now is all we have, so we must have faith and hope to make the Now tolerable. If your Now is bad, faith and hope do not suggest that you ignore the badness; they just tell you to do the best you can now, and that chances are tomorrow will be better. That's all, just look for a better tomorrow. I don't believe that blind ignorance is bliss, but I do believe that hope and faith can withstand any Now, no matter how terrible. Just suppose that in one of your Nows the worst befalls you: some criminal catches you off guard and dispatches you. That could happen, you know. You have chosen a very dangerous profession, and just as you can't understand how I keep my belief in an Ultimate Goodness, I can't imagine how a cynic like yourself decided that policing is worth the effort. Nevertheless, if in that last moment you have faith and hope, then you will not be disappointed; you will have died in a state of belief which no one can take from you. You will have died a happy man.

"And, I tell you this also, Frank O'Meara: happy saints are not found in the wealthy suburbs where these 'chosen' people live. And you have some notion that such places and such people exist, and you have contempt for them. Really, Frank, you're a grown man; you should know by now that the thing for which you have such overwhelming contempt does not exist. In fact, I think that somewhere, inside yourself, you do know and your contempt is just a disguise for the rage you feel at your own disappointment. No, Frank, there is no fairyland, and I submit to you that your skepticism is a thin veil for cowardice, specifically, fear of that very disappointment. Believe in nothing and you can't get hurt.

"The place where you think your brother lives is no place in this world. If Kevin does not bring God with him, it is because his head is in the wrong place, not his body. Sometimes I think that places like Chesterfield need my Carpenter more than this place here," he spread his hands and looked around. "In places like where your brother is, the need is better hidden, but it's there in a different form. It is so easy to ignore God when you are not suffering some great hunger, the absence of food, comfort, shelter, these things everyone needs, but not everyone gets. But having all the material comforts numbs you to your own purpose. If you become discontented, you are shamed into being still. After all, if you have a big house, a fine car, a nice family with healthy children, what more can you need? These things do not address a nagging emptiness that can never be acknowledged. Count yourself lucky, Frank, because every day of your life you are forced to question your Creator. What if you never thought of Him at all?"

They both sat there silently, Leon ruminating on his memories, Frank trying to follow the thread of Leon's logic. This long speech by Leon was the only time Frank had ever heard the man clearly and concisely explain his belief system. The last statement in particular, about being forced to think of God, had brought him up short, and he didn't know what to say. It certainly didn't explain the terrible things that happened to innocent people, while a God Who purported to love them stood idly by and allowed them to be eaten by monsters. On the other hand, Leon was right. There was a perverse comfort in the fact that yes, indeedy, he did think about God. Maybe not in very friendly terms, but probably more than his brother, Kevin, the priest, who sat in a comfortable rectory, had Sunday dinners with local politicos and high-powered CEO's, and never once thought it should be any other way. Somehow, in some way, he was better than his ordained brother, and the sense of failure he had brought into the mission with him was diminished.

Chapter Eight

While Sean Patrick O'Herlihy was facing Ray Stillwater in the garage, Anna Lee gently shook Jason, who was lying in the crook of her arm. They would go over to Father Leon's where he would wait in the back and she would eat and then bring out enough food for him. This would be the second time that they had done this, and she was beginning to feel like maybe she was successful in pulling the wool over Leon's eyes. She knew that he had looked at her yesterday morning, sensing something different about her, but she was sure he could not possibly know she was taking care of a young white boy. Maybe her step was a little lighter, a little more purposeful, but he could not know the cause of it.

She smiled into Jason's sleepy eyes and said softly, "C'mon, boy, let's go eat."

He stood up, donned his new headgear and put his hand into hers without question. She liked that, the way he trusted her so automatically. It made her feel like somebody, and she hadn't felt like somebody for a very long time. And for now, that would be enough. There would come a time when she would have to do the right thing, and give him up, but right now, in the constant struggle against the great enemy, Despair, let there be a little respite, let her have her moment.

As they got close to the mission, they separated without a word. Jason moved up the alley to the dumpster in back, and Anna Lee went inside to sit at the long, wobbly refectory table in the mission.

Actually, Leon had gotten it from one of the clothing manufacturers which used to populate this part of town. It was a big cutting table in its heyday, where skilled seamstresses and tailors laid out and cut designs for middle market customers. As the area began to deteriorate, and the big New York firms took over and moved manufacturing out of the United States, the buildings that housed valuable equipment like this were sold, torn down or abandoned. And sometimes, an alert priest could get a lot of good stuff if he could move fast and talk faster.

Right now, Leon was ladling out hot cereal this cold January morning. He stood behind the small steam table, using a large stainless steel ladle to dip out of a matching pot, smiling at the homeless, the toothless, the incoherent. He looked with gentle pleasure into each of the displaced faces, greeting them like honored guests. Anna Lee would have to be clever about getting some food out to Jason today. She saw a platter of buttered toast, and went for that, carefully carrying her Styrofoam bowl of cereal. She wouldn't eat all of it, because she knew that coming back for seconds would cause Leon to question her, or at least to look at her suspiciously.

She had always been very circumspect about the food she took, careful never to take more than her share, careful to make sure that everybody else had already had some if she did go back for seconds. Somehow, she would have to smuggle a half-full bowl of cereal and a pocketful of toast out to the back of the mission. If she was really lucky, she'd be able to get one of the oranges out, too. She knew that growing boys needed fresh fruit. She'd just wait until Leon's back was turned or he maybe left the room. He didn't just stand around and scrutinize his guests, she knew. So she'd wait her chance and get the food out to the boy.

Very shortly it came. As soon as Leon disappeared into his little office in the back, Anna Lee walked to the door, careful not to be too hurried. As she got to the door, she nonchalantly let her big coat sleeve fall over the bowl of cereal, and without a backward glance, she strolled at a leisurely pace around through the alley into the back to the dumpster. When she got there, she found Jason staring past her, wide-eyed, over her shoulder.

She handed the bowl to him and reached into her pocket for the toast, not understanding his gaze, until the voice behind her said, "Ah, so this is what you're up to, Anna Lee."

Anna Lee came within a hair of wetting her voluminous britches. Her hand froze in her pocket and she whirled to meet Leon's soft gaze, the smile playing around his mouth.

"Bring the boy inside, Anna Lee, where he can eat in the warmth, and we'll have a little talk, you and I," he said, and turned to go inside through the kitchen door.

He turned once and looked at her, still rooted to her spot, and said, "Well?" and then went inside.

Anna Lee sighed, looked at Jason, and said, "Well, I guess we've been busted, boy. Go on in, and wait for me in the dinin' room. I'll deal with Father the best way I can."

Jason followed along behind her, slurping hungrily out of the bowl, as Anna Lee trudged into the kitchen of the mission. She motioned him on into the dining room, where he went and got another bowlful of cereal, and she went back to Leon's office.

He was sitting in his swivel chair, and motioned toward the couch. "You want to tell me about it, Anna Lee?" he asked.

She rubbed her hand across her forehead

and said, "Not really, no, I don't, Father, but I guess I don't have much choice. Truth is, there's really not all that much to tell. The other night I woke up in the middle of the night, over there on my grate, you know, and there he was, standin' there in the streetlight. I thought at first I was, you know, hallucinatin' like I sometimes do, but I wasn't, he was real, and he was cold, and alone, and scared. So I did what my conscience told me to do, Father," and she looked over at him defiantly, defensively.

Leon knew about runaways and he knew about throwaway children. He had dealt with a few in his time, before the System (he always thought of the welfare system with a capital "S," like some sentient being) would step in and take over. The System was not adequate to the problems it encountered with these children. Sometimes they were institutionalized, but most frequently, they were forced to return to the homes they had left, homes where they were usually unwelcome and ill-treated. The System congratulated itself on another family, restored again, like some great victory had been won. All that happened was that, if the child could, he or she left again, and this time went underground to the predators who awaited their opportunities. The pathology of the family continued until somebody died, naturally or otherwise, and whatever children survived passed the mental sickness onto the next generation. The substance abuse, which was frequently at the bottom of the problem, continued on down the line.

These thoughts were all there, dancing peripherally around his central concern, which was Anna Lee. He knew her great heart, and was familiar with her disease. The good heart and the terrible illness had suffered through more than one confrontation within his view. The nobility that was the spirit of Anna Lee was caught in a chemical booby trap, and the possibilities of the situation with this boy made him sit straight up in his chair as she sat there and looked up at him from under her lowered cap.

He placed one of his hands over hers as she wrung them together. Leon's first impulse was to call Frank and get the Juvenile people over here - post haste. But some little voice in his head bade him be still, think a minute, before acting. He knew that Jason could certainly be in worse places, one of them being Juvenile Detention.

He smiled at Anna Lee, and said, "Anna Lee, we both know that you're courting a lot of trouble here, and if I help you, so am I. But for now, I have to tell you, I am in no great hurry to call the authorities in."

She raised her head up, joyous surprise on

her face. "I know, Father, I know I can't keep 'im, and I wouldn't even try, but, Father, just for a little bit." She put on her most earnest face. "This boy, Father, he's hurtin', and he needs a friend right now."

"I believe you, Anna Lee," Leon answered with equally serious mien. And he did. He knew that this extraordinary situation could only have been precipitated by the most uncommon events. But if a mess was coming, he wanted to know how many pairs of waders he was going to need.

He went to the door of the office, and looked around the dining room. Jason was almost alone at the table, scraping the bowl with the spoon, and looking around, presumably for further comestibles. He beckoned to the boy, holding up an apple. Jason rose without hesitation and came right for it. Leon gave him the apple and brought him into the office, shutting the door. Jason looked scared, but took a big bite anyway.

Leon held out his hand. "I'm Leon Devereux, Society of Jesus, and proprietor of this fine establishment. And you would be?" He waited expectantly, as Jason wiped his hand on his jacket and took Leon's for a brief manly shake.

"Jason Anglethwaite, sir," he said, looking up into Leon's face.

"Well, I am most pleased to make your acquaintance, Jason. Come, sit down here by Anna Lee, and tell me how you happen to be here." He gestured toward the couch as he moved to his swivel chair at the desk. He settled himself in and looked expectantly at the boy.

Jason looked back at him, then at Anna Lee. Evidently, he was reassured by what he saw, because he cleared his throat and began.

Alice Wright checked her appearance in the rearview mirror of her little red Ford Escort. She made sure her little African crown was in proper place, her hair neat. Then she turned to her right and gathered up her briefcase, once more checking the address on the form, comparing it to the one on the apartment building. Yes, right place. God, she hated this neighborhood. It reminded her of everything she had tried to escape from her past. Fortunately, it was cold weather, and no one sat on the front stoops to remind her of her origins, no target for her own self-loathing.

Alice Wright was a tall, slim black woman, respectable to the point of rigidity. She was always certain of the rightness of her position, she HAD to be right, it just couldn't be any other way. After all, with the aid of scholarships and grants she had managed to put herself through college, starting out first in the junior college system and then transferring to the University of Missouri-St. Louis campus, where she took her degree in Social Work, and then went back for her Master's in same. Nobody who wasn't right could have done that, given the obstacles in her path.

She had gotten good grades in elementary school, because she managed to come home in the afternoons and ignore her mother's drugged and drunken ravings, and somehow do the homework. If one of her mother's host of boyfriends (she had long since ceased calling them "uncle" or "daddy") breathed his hot liquor breath too close to her, she would somehow manage to evade his groping hands and continue to study. Alice knew she was better than this filthy little apartment that had been paid for by the taxpayers of Missouri.

She had never known her father, and didn't think that anybody was real sure who the daddies were of the four younger siblings, either.

If Alice had ever smiled, it was lost in the mists of time. She had nothing to smile about, in her life, or the world in which she lived it. She found out early that the most important thing was to keep a goal in front of her face, never looking to right or left. She was black, she was female, and where she came from, these were birth defects. She used to watch the caseworkers who made the obligatory calls to ensure no man was living in the apartment, do the food stamp and rental paperwork, and wonder at their stupidity. If another child was periodically added to the list, nobody ever really questioned why, or what Alice Wright's mother was doing. The general consensus was that everybody knew what caused babies, and if Effie Wright wanted to do that, then heaven forefend that her civil right to be promiscuous be abridged. Never mind that the babies were neglected and unsupervised, except by their older sister, Alice. Effie would beat Alice if one of the little kids got into enough trouble to interfere with her drinking and drugging. It was not that Effie was an uncaring person; she was so completely in the grip of her addictions that she could see nothing but satisfying their constant demands.

    Alice had a few memories of her mother as loving, concerned with her, even inconveniencing herself for Alice's needs. Life might have been easier for Alice if Effie had simply been completely terrible to her. The conflict in Alice's heart about her mother, whom she dearly loved, could have been relieved with the belief that Effie was simply no good. As it was, Alice knew that that was not the case. She never knew when the good mother was going to show up again, or what triggered her rare visits, but Alice always looked forward to seeing her and hoped for those times. She would do anything to please her, anything that she thought would bring the good mother out and keep her out, but as Effie's disease progressed, those times became rarer.

When Alice was thirteen years old, Effie overdosed on bad morphine and cheap port wine and was DOA at the old St. Louis City Hospital. Alice and her siblings were separated. The system was overloaded, underfinanced and indifferent to five more illegitimate black children and their emotional needs, so they were separated into various foster homes and Alice finished high school while living in the orphanage, acquitting herself well enough to win scholarships to the local branch of the state university, after attending a nearby junior college. Her determination to put Effie and everything about her behind a sealed door to the past solidified. She would NOT think about the mother she had both loved and hated, or the younger children; that only caused useless pain. She had no responsibilities here at the orphanage except her daily duties, and her studies. She applied herself diligently to the latter. She did not particularly like the nuns or the social worker. Whether or not they were likable people was immaterial; by this time Alice had decided somewhere deep inside that attaching her heart to others was a waste of time. The only person on whom she could depend was Alice, so be it. The rage was internalized and icebound.

As everything else in Alice's life came to be, she made her decision to take up social work based on things that she did not like. She had seen the failures of the system close up, she knew what was wrong, and she knew that she had the sense and the balls to fix it, if she could just get at it. Most people were fools, this she knew, particularly the white people who were in charge of just about everything. On the other hand, the black idiots who allowed themselves to be duped by the unscrupulous white people didn't have her respect, either. She viewed the entire human race from behind a glass wall in her mind which permitted her to see, but not to touch or to be touched. Much safer, when all that was on the other side were either imbeciles or criminals. She was proud of her isolation, which she called her "objectivity." She believed it allowed her to make the hard decisions, without any emotionalism involved. Things like compassion got in the way of what was good for everybody. She knew what was good for everybody, and she was going to make sure that they all got it, too, whether they wanted it or not. Now she knocked on the door of Lorraine Anglethwaite's apartment, already sure of what she would find. Another slatternly white woman, eyes red from crying over a mean drunk, and claiming that whatever was wrong with her children was not her fault, that she had done her best. As far as Alice was concerned, nobody but Alice ever did their best, and she felt nothing but contempt for their irresponsibility.

Frank sat in the doctor's office. He had called St. Louis University Hospital, and gotten the name of a urologist and same day service, dammit! When he described the symptoms the woman on the other end insisted. He hated being here! Not only was it a waste of time that could be spent doing his job, but what the hell good would it do anyway? Frank believed that if it was something important, no act of all the doctors in the AMA could fix it; if it wasn't, then he was just going to be embarrassed. This was terrible, and he was only doing it to keep Leon off his back.

Frank would have set his own hair on fire before admitting that he was scared right down to his hardworking leather soles. What if it was something awful? Everybody was gonna die anyway. Life was a well-known terminal condition, and nobody was getting out of it alive.

So? BFD! He looked at the toes of his shoes, a little scuffed where he had kicked his car door shut with his right foot in a childish snit, trying to tell himself that he was just aggravated looking for a parking place in the big underground garage attached to the hospital. The aggravation was the fact that he had found it.

Now he was here, and could think of no graceful way of backing out. God, now he was gonna have to pee in a cup, he just KNEW it. How humiliating. If the office nurse was young and pretty, he would die; if she looked like a lady biker, he would hate that even worse. Dammit, this was just unfuckingbelievable!

His mind went back over the years of chess/conversation/coffee with Leon. How had he ever gotten entangled enough to do something he hated so much just to please this person escaped him. Years of great conversation, yes; coffee, indifferent; chess, really bad. But, oh, that Leon, he could sell rowboats in the Sahara, and here he sat now. It all just seemed so unfair, somehow.

Sean Patrick O'Herlihy sat slumped on his side of the squad car, wishing they could take a beer break. Officer Phillips drove slowly up and down the streets of their beat, eyes peeled for anything, but mostly for a twelve-year-old blond boy who had taken off two days ago from a home where he no longer felt welcome. Phillips didn't particularly give a damn what O'Herlihy thought, felt or wanted; in fact, he was completely indifferent to his sulky presence. Phillips had long ago decided to do the best job he could, whether O'Herlihy wanted to or not. So Phillips whistled under his breath and kept looking.

Phillips slowed the car down, and pulled into the parking lot across the street from Jason's school. Sean sat up and looked at him inquiringly.

Phillips said, "I thought it might be a good idea to interview his teacher. She might have a clue about places where he could go."

Sean sighed. This was just so inconvenient, when a man needed a drink. He had been hoping that they would stop for coffee, and somehow he would get away from Phillips long enough to get some soul-warming alcohol down his gullet. Instead, Phillips, the Great Dedicated Cop, felt like he had to talk to teachers, or some such bullshit. Oh, well, they were here now, might as well go along with the program. They walked up the steps, excited children looking out the windows at the two uniforms coming into their school.

They walked into the office, where Phillips presented their credentials and were ushered into the principal's office. The principal then sent her secretary down to get Margaret Lewison out of class for a few minutes. Margaret came into the office, face pale, not knowing what to expect. The principal pulled a chair up for her, and allayed her fears about Fred and her children.

Wilson Phillips said, "I understand you're Jason Anglethwaite's teacher?"

"Yes, I am. Is anything wrong? I'm very fond of Jason, and if there is anything he needs, I would be glad to help."

"Well, frankly, Mrs. Lewison, Jason ran away from home night before last, and we're trying to locate him. A twelve-year-old boy has no business out away from home, especially in the dead of winter."

Margaret put her hand up to her cheek. "So that's why he hasn't been in class. I thought maybe he just had a cold, or something." She looked up at Phillips. "What happened?"

"Well, apparently there was some trouble with the stepfather, and Jason just ran out the door in the middle of the night. We were hoping that you could tell us where he might go, if he didn't want to sleep at home."

Margaret's eyes filled. "I'd hoped that he trusted me enough to come to me if it came to this. I guess he didn't. And I really don't know where he'd go. As far as I know, his only family is his mother and his little sister. His sister, Dodie, is here. She's in the third grade, but I don't believe she's been in class for the past couple of days, either." She paused, as the significance of that hit her. "Is Dodie okay?"

Phillips smiled, the warmth in his eyes reassuring to Margaret. "I have the impression that Mrs. Anglethwaite is so upset about Jason that she's afraid to let Dodie out of her sight. Whatever else is wrong there, I know she loves those kids."

He turned to the principal. "Does Jason have any friends he might confide in, someone who might know where he'd go?"

The principal in turn looked inquiringly at Margaret. "Jason was really a loner. He seemed all tied up within himself. We all knew that things weren't right at home, but we never really had anything substantive. And, besides, if you call the state, so much of the time their hands are tied. By the time DFS is able to act the child has died in an emergency room."

This last was said with a bitter downturn of her mouth. Her gaze hardened as she thought about the hypocrisy of a society that claimed to care, but refused to allocate the necessary funds for its most defenseless members. As a thirty-year veteran of the school system, she had seen it time and again, and was completely out of patience with excuses and simple indifference.

Phillips turned back to Margaret Lewison. "So he had no friends, nobody he'd talk to?"

"He played sometimes on the playground, but for the last few months, he was isolating more and more, sitting alone, ignoring the other children at recess. The only child he really talked to was Dodie. One time he got into a terrible fight with Richie Kazner, I don't know what set him off. But in detention I managed to talk him into working for me during the weekends this past fall." She looked up at Phillips. "In fact, until right around New Year's, he was over every weekend with Dodie in tow, doing little errands for my husband and me. We're really very fond of them both and would like to know that he's all right."

"Did you pay him money, Mrs. Lewison? Do you have any idea the amount he might have saved?"

"No, I don't. He averaged twenty to thirty dollars every weekend. He worked hard, and I paid him five dollars an hour. I don't know what he did with it, but I know what he didn't do - he didn't buy clothes or toys that I ever saw."

"So if he didn't spend it, he could have between two and three hundred dollars at his disposal, right?"

"Yes, I guess so, come to think of it. I

hadn't really realized it was that much money, but, yes, he could have that much."

Phillips paused and tugged at his earlobe, thinking. With that kind of funds, Jason could have gone to the Greyhound Bus station downtown and bought a ticket to God-knows-where, however far the money would take him.

Alice Wright laid the spoon on the saucer beside the coffee cup and smoothed her skirt. Then she reached into her briefcase and pulled out a clipboard with forms attached to it.

Across the room, Lorraine Anglethwaite waited in an old armchair. It should have been comfortable, but Lorraine was sitting on the edge of it, tension in every line of her body. She spoke calmly and softly in answer to Alice Wright's questions, but she was scared.

"If you would please fill out these forms, Mrs. Anglethwaite," Alice said.

Alice's face had no expression, so Lorraine could not read what she was feeling. Lorraine remembered her from the last time she had been here, when somebody from the school had sent the state over to see that her children were all right. That was several eternities ago, when Billy was still here, when she still had her son. She looked at the clipboard in her hand, and saw the questions: Jason's and Dodie's ages, whereabouts of their father, immunizations, school, etc., ad infinitum. Lorraine was puzzled by these questions, and looked inquiringly at Alice.

"What does their daddy have to do with all this? He's been gone seven years or better." She looked at Alice intently, trying to make sense out of the forms.

Alice stared back at her. God, what a wreck this woman was. Didn't these white women have any pride? Here she sat, smoking cigarette after cigarette, hair uncombed, old sweatshirt and jeans, no wonder her husband left seven years ago. "Mrs. Anglethwaite, the state is going to want to know a little bit more about this situation." She pronounced the word, "situation" as though it had hair on it that stuck in her mouth.

Lorraine said, "Miss Wright, you were here over a year ago. You already know all the answers to these questions. Ain't nothin' changed since then 'cept Billy Callahan don't live here no more, and I want my boy back."

These last five words came out low and carefully pronounced, as though she were talking to a lip reader. Alice did not know Lorraine well enough to recognize the signs of imminent danger. Lorraine's little clock was wound just about as tight as it could get, and it wouldn't take much more to spring it.

Alice Wright looked at Lorraine expressionlessly. "Mrs. Anglethwaite, this is the procedure. You must fill out these forms for me. If you don't want to, then I guess there's nothing left here for me to do." She gathered up her briefcase up and stood up.

Lorraine stood up with her. "Miss Wright, I don't know what it is that you all do over there in that child care department, or whatever that is that you work for. But I kin tell you this: I want my boy back, and I'll do anything to get 'im. To tell you the truth, I don't see that you have anything to do with bringin' 'im back, or anything useful at all. You come in here in your nice suit, and look all down your nose at me, and then act like I'm uncooperative 'cause I can't see that you're doin' anything for me or my boy." Her voice got lower, and she moved a step closer to Alice.

"Well, I'll fill out your damn papers, and I'll answer your damn questions, even though they're prolly none of your damn business. And then, Miss Fine-Lady Wright, if I don't see somethin' that counts towards gettin' my boy back, I'm gonna call somebody, I don't know who just yet, but I'll find out; I'm not as stupid as you think I am. Yeah, I'll call somebody and I'll find out just what it is that you do with all these answers to all these questions. And somehow, Miss Fancy Pants, I'll make your life real unhappy. I don't know how, and I don't know where, but I've had just about enough a 'thorities who come into my home, boss me around, and don't do nothin' fer me."

Lorraine's rage was beginning to make itself apparent physically; she was remembering the times her mother had begged for protection from her violent husband. She was remembering how her sister looked on the floor of her bedroom after Jack Daniels and painkillers had ended her short, unhappy life. Nobody had lifted a finger to help either Lorraine or her mother; the law was indifferent to protecting the likes of her; it just liked to push her around. She began to shake, and Alice Wright began feeling around in the chair behind her for her coat.

These trashy white women, the only way they knew how to handle problems was with violence. Alice drew herself up and said, "Mrs. Anglethwaite, I'm leaving. I'll leave these forms here for you, and when you recover yourself you can fill them out and mail them in." Alice was going to get out of here before this woman assaulted her, or whatever. What a waste of time these people were!

She detached the papers from the clipboard and laid them on the coffee table. Then she rummaged in her purse and brought up her business card, which she laid on top of the stack of papers. "You can mail them to me at this address."

She put her coat on and picked up her bag and briefcase and stalked out the door in a huff of offended dignity. Lorraine sank down on the couch, gathered a bewildered Dodie into her arms and wept some very old tears.

Chapter Nine

Jason and Anna Lee were both intently shelling peas for the soup Leon Devereux was making in the kitchen of the mission. Leon was cheerfully tasting and stirring the broth, jabbering away at Anna Lee and Jason about trivialities. His intent was to make them feel comfortable, and, for the moment, to distance them from the seriousness of their situation. There was nothing that could be done right at this moment, so until decisions were made, they might as well enjoy each other's company. Anna Lee kept her eyes on her flying fingers as she shelled peas.

Jason was a little more awkward, complicating his pea shelling progress by not being able to tear his eyes away from Leon for any appreciable length of time. He looked at the priest and was taken with his energy, his good nature, his intense joy of the moment. Here, in this clean, bright kitchen, this tall black man, who might have been African royalty, seemed to be thrilled with the kingdom he had, a kingdom of untouchables. Madmen with unseeing eyes, disillusioned men with bitter, suspicious eyes wandered in and out of Leon's domain. To each one he gave his individual attention, listening to each tale, no matter how trivial, no matter how fantastic, giving each the weight the teller felt he deserved. A word of thanks was rare from any of King Leon's subjects, yet he continued to reign cheerfully and willingly. Of course, Jason was not sophisticated enough to verbalize these ideas, but he understood that Leon gave mightily of himself, and never ran out of patience. Jason had never seen a man act like this before. Most of his experience with adult males had been with Billy; he could barely remember his father. Mr. Lewison, his teacher's husband, was a nice man, but Jason had never really felt that he could confide in him. With Leon, however, he felt a trust, a sense that whatever happened, Leon would do the very best he could for Jason.

As Leon continued his stream of happy chatter, glad to have company to help him in the kitchen, they heard a heavy footstep from the front, and a loud "Hey, Lee, anybody home?" from the front of the mission.

Leon froze, then looked at Jason. "Go upstairs, son. Right now, this is the best way."

Anna Lee looked up at the priest, the gratitude on her face shining. Jason fled into the corridor and up the stairs, not really sure where he was going. He had not been upstairs yet, and had no idea what to expect. But he understood that the priest would never direct him to anything wrong or dangerous.

Leon poked his head out the kitchen door into the dining room of the mission and hollered, "I'm in here, Frank."

Frank O'Meara turned in the direction of the kitchen. He pulled a chair out from the rickety old table, and slipped his coat across the back. He then went to the cabinet and took out a thick white mug that had survived only-God-knew-what, and filled it from the coffee urn. Then, going back to the table sat down and smiled at Anna Lee. She looked up at him, grinned shyly back, and continued with her pea shelling.

"Well, say, Anna Lee, it's good to see you here. Ya' helpin' ol' Leon here? Ya know, he can't rest until he's gotten everybody to pitchin' in to this money pit, can ya, Lee."

Leon turned around, a rather ludicrous sight in his priestly collar, with white chef's apron over it, a large wooden spoon in his right hand. This latter he brandished threateningly, and made a mock gesture of hitting Frank on the head with it.

"You, too, could do some good around here, especially considering the amounts of coffee you guzzle." He was secretly very glad to see Frank in such apparent high spirits. He wanted to ask him about their discussion of the other day, and if Frank had made an appointment to see a doctor.

Frank hooked his toe around the other kitchen chair, dragging it close, and rested his heel on the rung. He leaned back and laced his fingers behind his head and grinned, saying nothing. Anna Lee continued shelling, fingers flying as they had once flown over ivory keys.

Leon removed his apron and got a twin to the cup Frank was cuddling between his palms. After filling it from the urn, he sat down at the table with Frank and Anna Lee and said, "So, what brings the long arm of the law here tonight?"

Frank stretched a little, and said, "Oh, nothing in particular; just looking for a little game of chess. Of course, I could beat you blindfolded, but I thought I'd maybe give you a break and let you see what you can do."

Leon laughed softly and said, "You couldn't beat a three-year-old if you had four eyes and a manual. But after dinner, I'll take you on and show you how this game is properly played. You will eat with us, won't you, Frank?"

At this Anna Lee looked up, alarm on her face. This was not lost on Frank, who returned her gaze quizzically. Leon hastily interjected, "It's all right, Anna Lee, there is enough." He knew she was worried about Jason, if he'd have to stay upstairs much longer. Anna Lee was no fool. She knew the dormitory was upstairs, and she wasn't altogether comfortable with the men who normally slept up there. She didn't want Jason up there on his own for too long.

Leon understood her fear, and said, "Back in a minute, Frank. I've got to go upstairs and check on a drunk who came in this afternoon. Anna Lee, if you will, keep an eye on the soup kettle for me, I'll be right back."

Reassured, Anna Lee nodded and went over to the great kettle simmering on the stove. Leon went out of the room and up the back staircase of the mission.

There were two staircases, but he kept the door to the back one locked and carried the only key. It was through this door that he entered the dormitory and saw Jason sitting on one of the iron cots, looking out the window into the gray evening sky. There was no one else in the room with him, and in his solitude the loneliness and sadness showed on his young face. Leon's heart went out to him, and all the children who were unappreciated and unwanted. He sat down on the cot next to Jason, close enough to be reached if Jason wanted to reach out, but far enough away not to violate his space.

"Jason, we have a policeman who is going to stay here with us this evening; he will have dinner here and afterwards, he and I will play some chess. We do this frequently, and I can't think of any way of putting him off without arousing his suspicions. Do you think you will mind eating up here alone?"

Jason shook his head, looking down at his hands in his lap. His misery was so apparent and Leon felt so helpless in the face of it

"Jason," he began awkwardly, "I know that this is an uncomfortable situation for you, but this is what life on the run is like. The sooner we can make your whereabouts known and your presence here legal, the better." He lifted Jason's chin with his thumb and forefinger and directed the boy's gaze to himself. "You know that I would never do anything to jeopardize you, don't you, Jason? I will keep your confidence unless I am absolutely assured that to continue to do so would hurt you worse than breaking it would."

Jason nodded, tears in his eyes. He had been wondering what his mother was doing right now, and if Dodie missed him. Maybe she did, but probably not his mom. She had that crazy-ass Billy, and she was probably glad he was out of the way. The pain in Jason was growing, writhing in his chest, twisting to get out, and he gulped to keep it down. That did nothing but briefly postpone the terrible moan that escaped from him, an agonizing sound that went straight to Leon's heart. His arms went around the boy, who sat stiff and unrelenting. Leon understood that he was ashamed, and began to gently stroke his hair. Suddenly, Jason turned his face into Leon's chest and began to make great choking sobs that filled the room. Leon, somewhat alarmed that this would be heard by some of the sharper ears in the building, began to gently shush Jason. The intensity gradually lessened until he was only making those shivering sighs that come after hard crying.

Leon gently released him. "I must go back downstairs. Anna Lee will be up soon with your supper." He softly closed the door behind him. As he entered the kitchen, Frank O'Meara raised his eyebrows and made exaggerated glances at his wristwatch.

Leon said, "My drunken friend is not feeling so well," discouraging any further conversation.

Anna Lee was stirring the soup pot and looked inquiringly at Leon. "Anna Lee," he said, "In a little bit, would you please take some soup up to our sick friend?"

Anna Lee nodded, and Leon began to get out the assorted dinnerware that he used in the dining room, some of which he had bought at rummage sales, some of which he had simply no memory of how it had been acquired. It nonetheless served the purpose, and he set it out as proudly as if it were complete gold-plated service for a state dinner.

"Prepare yourself for humiliating defeat, Frank," he said, smiling like a shark as he carried plates, bowls, etc., on a large tray into the dining room through the swinging door.

Sean Patrick O'Herlihy stared at his stocking feet, propped on the coffee table in his tiny living room. He held a bottle of beer in his right hand, elbow resting on the arm of the sofa. He was wondering if little Rookie Rita was busy tonight, and if he'd had the sense God gave to small animals, he would have gotten her phone number the other night. But he'd forgotten; in fact, there was a lot about that night that he simply could not remember, but, aw, what the hell. Everybody forgot stuff. But this led to the uncomfortable realization that there was something important he'd forgotten, something that nagged on the edges of consciousness, something that Big Bad Ray and his sidekick, what's-his-face, knew and Sean did not. He remembered the encounter in the garage that morning, which he still could not figure out.

This, then, led to another, even more unpleasant thought: He was at least ten years older than Big Bad Ray and what's-his-face, and yet, he still had the same rank. He was still a patrolman, had never made sergeant, would never, it seemed like, make detective. He'd taken the tests several times, and each time failed, borderline, but failed just the same. Sean felt that the department could cut him some slack, but just wouldn't. Further proof of what assholes he was surrounded by. He was a good cop, and they knew it. They were just jealous, and they were gonna keep him down.

He drained off the last of the beer, and went to the fridge for another. There was only one more, and Sean knew that before an hour was up, he was going to have to go to Walgreen's and correct that situation. Well, that was okay. Beer was the only friend he had in this rotten, fucking world, and he wasn't going to turn away from the only buddy he had ever known. His mother had abandoned him, his father abused him and deserted him by dying; the nuns had mistreated him, and his wife was a faithless bitch. He was partnered with a self-righteous suckup nigger who tap-danced his way up the ladder, while everybody applauded Step 'N' Fetchit Wilson, fuckin' Uncle Tom.

Sean's notion of justice had nothing to do with examining his input into his circumstances. Everybody was unfair to him, he had been singled out by an unkind Fate to suffer through a miserable life, and then die. That there were people worse off than he only confirmed his belief that God, whoever or whatever else He was, was an arbitrary bastard, and it was no use trying to play by the rules, because the Almighty was likely to change them in the middle of the game, and then punish you for not knowing the new ones. Questions that baffled him as a child were never answered. There was no stability in the world, nobody in charge could be trusted, so a person could only live by depending on himself. If Sean had once had a hope, a belief in something beautiful, it had been thoroughly trampled by the time he was twelve years old. It was safer by far to nurse resentment than take the risk of trust.

He got off the couch, and went to the closet to get his jacket and then realized that he didn't have any shoes on. As he leaned over to get them, he staggered, then completely lost his balance and banged his head ferociously on the corner of the coffee table. He just lay there on the floor, hand over his right eye, blubbering drunkenly.

While Frank and Leon merrily tried to outwit each other at the chessboard, Anna Lee and Jason stayed upstairs. Anna Lee took the opportunity to strip Jason down and wrap him in a blanket, and took his clothes into the basement for a quick wash and dry. Leon's old washing machine still ran pretty quietly, but the dryer was given to strange sounds.

Although Anna Lee moved quietly, always a surprise, given her size, the racket from the dryer startled Leon and Frank, and Frank automatically reached for his holster under his arm.

Leon reached his hand over and said, "It's only my old clothes dryer, Frank. I think my drunk is coming to himself and trying to get his clothes clean. Maybe I'd better go check."

He got up and, to Frank's utter astonishment, fairly ran to the kitchen towards the basement door. Once there, he saw Anna Lee poking around in the dryer.

"Anna Lee, what are you doing?" he asked.

"Oh, sorry to disturb you, Father, but I wanted to get Jason some fresh clothes. Y'know, he's been in the same ones for two days, and I don't think that's so good for the boy."

Leon smiled. "And you're exactly right, Anna Lee. However, Frank O'Meara is getting the wind up here, and sooner or later, he's going to ask some uncomfortable questions."

"Oh, Father, does he know?" Anna Lee looked stricken.

Leon walked over to her in front of the

dryer. "You know, Anna Lee, you are going to have to give the boy over. You can't keep him much longer."

He spoke tenderly, gently. He was becoming genuinely alarmed at what would happen when they were finally separated.

Anna Lee quietly said, "I know that, Father. I know. I just," she scratched behind her ear as she searched for words. "I just wanted him to have a little time to feel loved."

She raised her eyes to the priest, who, at six feet, two inches, was one of the few people around who stood over her.

"I just wanted to give him somethin' to take down the road with 'im. Ya see what I'm sayin'?"

Once again, Leon marveled at the heart of this woman. A stranger looking at her would see a caricature of a human being, a bloated, glassy-eyed figure, much like the huge cartoon balloons flown for the Thanksgiving Day parades. It took some exposure to her to understand that while she certainly was impaired in a significant way, this defect had never found its way into her heart, which remained pure, innocent and wise.

Leon put an arm around her stooped shoulders and said, "Come, Anna Lee, take the boy's clothes upstairs to him, and hang them over the radiator. I'll be up in a little while, and after

Frank leaves, if they're not dry by then, we'll put them into the dryer."

At the top of the steps Leon opened the door to the kitchen, and whispered to Anna Lee, "Let me go first. I will keep Frank occupied and you hotfoot it back upstairs."

She nodded and they parted ways.

Sean Patrick O'Herlihy left Walgreen's carrying a fresh twelve-pack. He lost his footing and stumbled, cursing. It interfered with his thought processes, and he was on the trail of a hot one. In a flash of incredible brilliance (hah! that asshole Phillips could never think like this), he had discovered what was wrong: he needed the opportunity to demonstrate what he was made of. He was the stuff of legends, by God, he was. He wasn't just a good cop, he was a fucking **GREAT** cop, and by Christ, it was about time those fuckers at the stationhouse knew it. All he needed was the right situation, the right scenario, and he'd by God show 'em, he would. He was in the process of sifting through various possibilities when he tripped over the sidewalk, and interrupted his planning. Never mind, he, the great cop, Sean Patrick O'Herlihy, could rise above all this; no sidewalk was going to get him down, and he began to strut jauntily to the front door of the four-family flat where he occupied three rooms on the downstairs left.

Chapter Ten

DAY THREE, January 31st Another day broke exactly like the previous one: bright, clear and cold. It was the last day of January, ice was glittering on the pavement and wind was whipping through the St. Louis streets. Early risers were already outside, especially in the suburbs, cranking cold engines, and AAA was gearing up for a deluge of calls to revive dead batteries. The morning news informed whoever was listening that, while it was not record cold, at minus five degrees Fahrenheit, it was damned cold by anybody's reckoning.

Frank O'Meara was shaving and wondering about Leon's unusual behavior the night before. It wasn't any one thing, but a syndrome of things; Leon almost never left their game, unless it was a real emergency. He usually valued a couple of hours of recreation in the evening, what he called his "down time." In fact, he needed it to continue the next day. Why, then, did he run down the basement and upstairs, more than once? Not only did he leave in an uncharacteristic way, but he was very reticent about why.

Furthermore, Frank had never known Anna Lee to spend an entire night in any mission on the Row, no matter what the weather. As for helping Leon cook, there should have been a national holiday declared! Anna Lee, in an apron, helping with supper at Leon's mission house! What the hell had been going on over there? It had bothered him so much that he had abandoned the real purpose of his visit, which was to tell Leon that he had been to the doctor that day. Oh, well, today, he would drop by early and tell Leon and at least put that much to rest. Maybe he could also get a line on yesterday's peculiar behavior.

Sean Patrick O'Herlihy was nursing another hangover, something he barely noticed anymore. It was like an old friend he would have missed had it not appeared. He knew just what to do: two cups of strong coffee and eight Excedrin supplied enough caffeine and pain killer to get him through the morning. During the past month he'd also discovered another ingredient was really helpful in his coffee. Just a little touch of Wild Turkey really seemed to hit the spot, stop the shakes. It took care of the gray ragged edges, and he could face another day with the virtuous Wilson Phillips, another twenty-four hours of knowing he should be further along career-wise than he was. He poured his first cup of coffee, dropped about a half shot of bourbon into it, and took the Excedrin. Then he poured himself the second cup, with the rest of the shot, and kicked back at the kitchen table, putting his feet up. His bitch of an ex-wife would never let him do that, until one morning he got sick of her naggin' and raggin', and simply backhanded her. That night when he got home, the locks had been changed and two paper bags holding his underwear were on the front stoop, his shaving kit on top. Well, to hell with that cunt. A man is allowed to put his feet onto his own table in his own house, and no bitch of an ex-wife could tell him otherwise.

Right now, his priority was getting the attention he'd decided last night he deserved. He would have to be really alert, watching for any opportunity to take down a criminal, help an officer, even set up a situation, if necessary. In fact, he might even go so far as saving St. Wilson's black ass, if it came to that. Oh, shit, wouldn't that be a joke on them both. He swung his feet off the table, ground out his cigarette, grabbed his jacket and left, ready to prove his mettle.

Alice Wright awoke with a splitting headache, which was a common event since she was about six years old; it had, of late, become almost a daily thing. She never slept well, she'd wake up with her jaws clenched, and some painful memory of her childhood with Effie would replay itself in her mind, unbidden and heedless of her demand that it go away. She sometimes wished that she could cry, but she actually saw no reason to. Crying was for weaklings and simps, something she certainly was not. Last night the tape had run several of the times Effie had used the belt on Alice because the younger children had somehow inconvenienced her; Alice had failed to keep them properly under control because she was too busy studying, or changing a diaper, or cleaning up a mess. Effie, drunk and screaming, would strip her down and bend her over the kitchen table. She always left raw welts on Alice's back. Once a teacher at school had seen them, and had dragged Alice into the girls' bathroom, demanding to see more clearly what she had noticed through Alice's thin cotton blouse. Alice, still as a stone statue, let the woman look. When finished, she asked Alice how she'd gotten them. Alice was also as mute as a stone statue. The teacher realized that nothing she did here would do any good. The silent tears began to trickle down her little face, and the teacher grabbed her to her breast, tears coming to her own eyes. The teacher, however, was very wary of the welfare system, so she simply told Alice if she ever needed any help, she would be there for her. She wrote her number down on a piece of paper, and as the class filed out of the room for the last time that day, handed it to Alice. Alice never used it. She was already beyond believing anybody.

She went into the bathroom and looked into the mirror as she reached for her toothbrush. Her eyes were bloodshot, so when she got out the toothpaste, she also took out some Visine in the hopes that eye drops, combined with her large dark glasses, would prevent the questioning looks she always got after a night like this last one. Alice knew she was strong, and that she would not give in to the memories. She would achieve, she would do the best job possible, she would leave her stamp on the world. She knew that her will was what had kept her going, and it would continue to keep her going, maybe up to a directorship in the agency. However, temporarily, it might not hurt to see a doctor about some sleeping pills. She couldn't be going into work looking like she had a hangover. She never touched a drop.

Lorraine Anglethwaite likewise had not slept so well, either. She would wake up and wonder about Jason, if he was cold, if he was hungry, where he was, why he wasn't here, and then she'd cry herself into a light doze, just as she had done the night before. Dodie was sleeping next to her, soundly, but with a lot of thrashing about, but that was something you expected with little kids.

As light came through the bedroom window Lorraine quietly swung her legs off the bed and felt around on the floor for her slip-ons. She picked up her cigarettes from the nightstand, turned and looked at Dodie. God, her baby. Where was her other baby? Oh, God, please look after my boy, better than I did, please, God. Then she padded out into the kitchen and made herself a cup of instant coffee, lighting up a cigarette, and crying a little more. Today she would fill out those damned forms for that snotty black woman. Why were they always so snotty? Why did they always look at her like she was something found on a used tissue? She was sick to death of them, sick to death of this apartment, sick to death of her life. When she finally got Jason back (she refused to entertain the possibility that she mightn't), there would be some changes.

She sat there, watching the clock until it was time to call into work, and ask for another personal day. She didn't care whether she got it or not; they could fire her ass, she didn't care. She just wanted her boy back.

At the mission, Leon had arisen at four-thirty; he went quietly into the small chapel and celebrated his usual private daily mass. This was for him, this was his time with his God, and nothing was going to interfere with it. This was the font from which he drank, this time of day with his Father. By five-thirty he was in the kitchen, quietly preparing breakfast for his guests.

By six o'clock, Anna Lee was awake and washing up. Then she gently woke Jason and wiped his sleepy face down with a warm soapy cloth.

"Here, baby, you just be still and let Anna Lee wipe your face. You got dirty, boy, messin' aroun' waitin' for me in the alley."

Very tenderly, she wiped the soap off, and stroked his blond hair. Then she pulled him up into her arms like a baby. Jason was tall enough, but small boned, and Anna Lee lifted him as easily as a puppy. She wrapped a blanket around him and carried him down into the kitchen. She wanted to personally oversee his breakfast.

Leon saw her come in with the boy and started to tell her to carry him into the dining room, but she beat him to the punch.

"I want to feed my boy here, Father. It's like, I dunno know, a little personal service I can do for him." She set him down in the old wooden chair in the kitchen and started getting out Cream of Wheat, a pot which she filled with water, milk and butter.

"Anna Lee, don't you think you should..." He was cut short.

She looked up at him and said, "Father, I know what you're gonna say, and I know it's for my own good. But I need to do this, Father, I really do. I know, I know better than you, that I'm gonna have to give him up. With every passin' day, it gets closer. So while I got 'im, lemme do this, so I don't have any regrets when they take 'im away from me." Her eyes were very clear this morning, clear and piercing in their gaze.

Her shoulders were as straight as Leon had ever seen them and he nodded his head once, wordlessly acquiescing to her will. She went on about fixing Jason's breakfast, while the boy watched with sleepy eyes, head resting on the heel of his hand, propped by his elbow.

Leon was humming a little tune, starting the coffee, when the kitchen door opened. At first he thought the cold blast of wind that accompanied it was the culprit, then he looked up and saw Frank O'Meara standing in the doorway. Frank was standing there, looking closely at Jason's sleepy face, stock still.

Then he looked at Leon and said, "I've seen this boy's face on a flyer at the stationhouse."

Leon looked guiltily at the floor. "Frank, I was going to let you in on our little secret. In fact, I was going to ask your advice. We just wanted a little time to decide how to approach this thing." He looked up at Frank, pleading in his eyes, a apologetic smile on his lips.

Frank said, "Leon, I have never known you to break the law. You're the most scrupulously honest person I've ever met. What's goin' on here?"

Leon got up and got a cup down for Frank, and refilled his own. He nodded to Anna Lee, and she continued getting Jason's breakfast. Then he launched into the story of Jason.

Frank listened quietly, and then said, "Well, you know that we have to abide by the rules here. But I can make it easier for you, and that's what I'll do."

He turned to Anna Lee's back and said, "Anna Lee, I'm going to see what I can do for you down at the stationhouse, but you and Jason have to stay here with Lee. No going back out on the street, you understand?"

Anna Lee turned around and said, "Oh, no, sir, Mr. O'Meara. We're gonna stay right here 'til you tell us what to do."

Then she put down the spoon onto the stove and walked over to Frank and stood over him. She stuck out her long-fingered hand and said, "And I want to thank you, Mr. O'Meara, for bein' patient and listenin' to Father Leon here, and not just runnin' off and gettin' some caseworker to come in here and take Jason away without findin' out what's best for everybody concerned. That's considerate of you, and I want to thank you."

Frank accepted the outstretched hand, shook it, and then shook his head. "Anna Lee, you're a wonder, you surely are."

Then he looked at Leon. "Mainly, Lee, I came by to tell you." he shot a look towards Anna Lee, but she was already herding Jason upstairs with the breakfast tray. Nevertheless, he dropped his voice. "I came by to tell you that I went to the doctor yesterday. I wanted to tell you last night, but you were so busy runnin' in and out and upstairs and downstairs and I got so interested in all the excitement, I just forgot."

Leon laughed. "Well, now you know. Jason was here last night with Anna Lee, and we were trying to decide the best course of action for them. And, Frank, I must say, I am delighted to hear that you have done the sensible thing. You should have results back very shortly, and then we'll know what to do from there. I shouldn't have to tell that you will be in my prayers today. Of course, you are every day, but today, there will be a special effort for you." His eyes twinkled. "Maybe today I will once again call on Augustine. He is special to me, and might do you some good."

The "we" in was not lost on Frank. He knew that his good friend would involve himself in Frank's health concerns, and that if he, Frank, tried to stop him, it would really insult Leon. The priest could be like an old woman when somebody he cared about was at stake. And Frank decided right then that maybe that wasn't such a bad idea, to let Leon in on this. Sometimes you need a friend.

Patrolman Sean Patrick O'Herlihy sat slumped in his usual position in his corner of the squad car while Sgt. Wilson Phillips drove. Today, he didn't care that St. Wilson was driving, or where he went. For the first time in a long time, Sean Patrick O'Herlihy was a Man with a Plan. He was going to be a hero, and, by God, somebody was going to notice that he was one damned good cop. All he had to do was keep his eyes peeled and his ears open. Staying slumped down in the seat was part of the Plan. If he sat up and looked straight ahead, Phillips would know something was up, because Sean always slumped down in the seat. Maybe Phillips would even guess that Sean was on the alert for lawbreakers. Whether he did or not, Sean's alert posture would, in turn, alert Phillips, and then Sean's glory would be stolen by this nigger dirtbag. It was **NOT** going to happen. Phillips had coasted along on Sean's coattails long enough. The time had come for Sean to collect his due, and, by God, he was gonna. Watch out, you motherfuckin' criminals, Sean Patrick O'Herlihy was comin', and he was loaded for bear.

    Frank sat at his desk at the stationhouse, looking at the flyer with Jason's face on it. He went over to Rick Jankowski and said, "Rick, do you know who caught this job?" He laid the flyer down on Jankowski's desk.
    Jankowski picked it up and looked at it. "I think the uniforms took it, Frank. They're better equipped to deal with it, bein's they're out on the street all the time. I thought I saw Phillips and O'Herlihy pick it up the other day."
    Frank said, "Oh, brother. Whatever O'Herlihy touches turns to shit. If Phillips weren't right on top of 'im, God knows what he'd do."
    Jankowski nodded in the affirmative. Everybody knew that O'Herlihy had an attitude problem, and occasionally had to be restrained by Phillips when stopping a suspect. There had also

been the occasional rumor of money changing hands where O'Herlihy was concerned. Nothing had ever been proved, but the rumor was enough. Most of the men on the police force were decent, honest men. Over the years, they might become a bit cynical, but most of them lived on their salaries. The bad cop was the exception. But he got all the publicity, and the honest ones objected to being tarred with the same brush as guys like O'Herlihy.

Worse than that, there had recently been a very nasty rumor about him and a female rookie; the word "rape" had been whispered at the coffee machines. There had been no charges filed, but the women on the force would fall silent when O'Herlihy walked into the stationhouse, and one of the female detectives had said loudly that "the smell of something dead just blew in" on one occasion when Sean came in. Sean hadn't even picked up on it, although if he had, everybody was ready.

Frank said, "Do you know if they've had any luck, Rick?"

"I don't think so. You know how it is with runaways, Frank; they just kind of disappear into the night until they turn up in an alley or the river floatin' face down."

Frank said, "Has Social Services been called in?"

Jankowski suddenly looked up. "Well, Frank, I'm not sure, but you can find out easy enough. What's your interest in this anyways? You're Homicide, aren't you?"

Frank shrugged and said, "I thought I saw him downtown around skid row; just thought I'd give Phillips the info, if he wanted it."

Jankowski turned around in his chair and hollered at one of the women at the filing cabinet. "Hey, Vera, has Social Services been called on the Anglethwaite kid?"

Vera, who was one of the juvenile officers, left the filing cabinet in which she'd been rummaging, and went to another. She pulled out a manila folder. Thumbing through it, she looked up and said, "Yeah, Alice Wright has that one."

Jankowski looked back up at Frank. "Okay, happy now?"

Frank laughed and said, "Yeah, thanks, Rick."

He went over and asked Vera if he could see the file. She looked at him quizzically over her glasses, but didn't argue. Frank had seniority, and moreover, a lot of respect at the stationhouse. Frank took the file over to his desk, opened it and found Alice Wright's phone number at the Missouri Social Services, Children's Division. All he could get was her voicemail, so he left a message, set the file aside, and went on with some of the endless paperwork that was part of a cop's lot.

About an hour later, his phone rang and he picked it up. "O'Meara," he said into the mouthpiece.

"Detective O'Meara?" asked a female voice.

"That's what I said, I'm O'Meara."

There was the briefest of silences, and then the female voice said, "I'm Alice Wright, Det. O'Meara. I'm returning your call."

"Oh, yeah. Thank you, Miss Wright. I wanted to talk to you about Jason Anglethwaite."

A note of caution was discernible in Alice Wright's voice. "What about Jason Anglethwaite, Det. O'Meara?"

"Well, I think I might have a line on him, but I'd really need to see you and the officers on the case. Maybe we could set up a meeting, you, me, Officers Phillips and O'Herlihy, for tomorrow. Would that be convenient?"

"Well, I'm not sure convenience is the issue. I'm sure I don't have to tell you, Det. O'Meara, that if you know anything about the boy or his whereabouts, you need to tell me immediately, so that we can get him home."

Frank spoke very carefully. "I'm sure that we all have the boy's best interests in mind, Miss

Wright. Do you think we could meet tomorrow?"

There was a moment's silence during which he heard the riffling of pages. "I could make it about one-thirty tomorrow afternoon. Where do you want to meet?"

Frank said, "Right here, at the precinct. I'll make sure that Phillips and O'Herlihy are here, too. Thank you very much, Miss Wright." He was talking to a dead line. She had already hung up

Chapter 10

DAY FOUR, February 1st The next day, February first, dawned exactly as its predecessors: sunny and Arctic-frigid. On his way to the stationhouse, Frank stopped at Leon's mission to tell him that he would be meeting that day with the officers in charge of the case and the social worker assigned to it. He felt that, if handled right, everybody could go home satisfied.

After roll call, before they went to the garage, the watch commander called Phillips and O'Herlihy aside. Sean was very glad that he had just slathered on some more aftershave; he didn't think anybody could tell, but it's always best to be safe.

He was unaware that Phillips, who could and did smell him, was just waiting for the right time to turn him in for drinking on the job. Unfortunately, he could never catch him in the act, but the smell alone would knock you over. Phillips thought that maybe this was the chance he'd been waiting for.

To his regret, it wasn't. The watch commander seemed bowled over by Sean's aftershave, and told him to stop wearing so much, he "smelled like a friggin' perfume counter." Then he got to the real reason he wanted to talk to them: They were to come in off the streets at one-thirty today and report to Frank O'Meara. There was something going on about the Anglethwaite kid, and Frank needed to speak to them.

Sean was thinking inside his own head, "Big whoopdedoo!" Phillips' curiosity was excited: why would a plainclothes detective be involved in this? In any case, they'd be there.

Alice Wright sat down at her desk at eight a.m. sharp, as she always did. She didn't actually need to be there until eight-thirty; however, she liked to get an early start. Besides, it looked good.

She checked her calendar and wondered why a police detective needed to talk to her about a runaway. Had they found the child's body? God, she had so wanted to take him back to his mother. It would look so good on her record: another family reunited. The state and her superiors liked that.

If he was dead, there could be problems. It was in the record that she had been called in about that family before, and if it looked like she had been in any way negligent, she would be the fall guy. Nobody would ever stand up and say that the System encourages the caseworkers to keep families together, even if they're tying the kids up and locking them in the basement without food for weeks at a time. There were, of course, no formal guidelines to this effect. But the informal power structure really liked it when kids were left in their homes with their biological parents. If it turned out that the biological parents were savages, then the caseworkers were the shock absorbers for their superiors and the judges who insisted that only a biological mother was capable of raising her offspring. So Alice was seriously concerned about her unblemished record. After today, would it still be unblemished?

The morning crept by for O'Meara, Phillips and Wright. O'Herlihy didn't give a damn, except insofar as this meeting interfered with his Plan. If he were in the stationhouse instead of on the street, how could he be a hero? If he were a hero, he could go to Clancy's and stand everybody drinks, but nobody would ask him for money.

O'Meara wanted to get this business done. He wasn't happy about this situation; it reeked of conspiracy, and he was in the middle. This was the kind of thing the news media would be all over, if something went wrong with that kid. Leon and Anna Lee would do everything in their power to take care of him, but Superman's just a comic book hero. He doesn't exist in real life, and Frank knew all about the best laid plans of mice and men.

Phillips was just really curious about what was going on.

Wright, like O'Meara, wanted it over with, also. She wanted to know how much trouble she was in so she could start taking whatever CYA action was necessary.

Finally, it was one-thirty. Frank filled a carafe with fresh coffee and took it and some paper cups, sugar and cream envelopes with stirrers and napkins on a tray into the little conference room. It wasn't much, an old table and some folding chairs, but it would afford privacy, and the coffee made Frank look affable.

The first arrival was Alice Wright. Frank stood up, put on his brightest smile and extended his hand. She ungloved her right hand and gave it to him. It was limp. Frank, however, kept smiling and took her coat, then escorted her into the conference room.

He was just coming back into the squad room when Phillips and O'Herlihy came in with the cold February day all over them. Frank could smell the cold on Phillips, but thought he was getting a whiff of something else from Sean, and didn't like it. Of course, he didn't like Sean, he never had. Even so, he tried not to let his prejudices make his decisions for him, and he needed for this meeting to move on. "Over here," he motioned with his arm.

The two uniforms hung up their jackets, and were heading for the big coffee pot. Frank hollered, "I've got some fresh coffee in here, guys. Come on."

They made their way between the desks. Phillips came in, nodded to Alice Wright, and sat down. Sean grabbed a chair, turned it around backwards, and, placing his hands on the back of it, rested his chin on them. Frank noted the Band-Aid on Sean's right eyebrow, and wondered if one of his host of ill wishers had finally caught up with him. However, he kept a bland expression, concealing his dislike of Sean. He wasn't too sure he liked Alice Wright, either. He had seen her around the precinct several times, and he always felt that if this woman deviated the least bit, she would shatter. There was a tension in her posture, her bearing and her gestures, that made him very watchful. Frank then sat down himself and started filling coffee cups, much like the lady of the manor at teatime.

Everybody got theirs, with or without, whatever their preference, and Frank leaned back and sipped his. The other three faces turned toward him inquiringly.

"I have a line on the Anglethwaite boy, but before I give out any information, I have to tell you, I want some promises from you." He turned his head. "In particular, from you, Miss Wright."

Alice Wright sat very still. "Det. O'Meara, as I indicated on the phone yesterday, I'm sure that you know the law. If the boy is being detained by anyone other than his parents, I will see that action is taken against you." Nobody, not even this hotshot white detective, was going to interfere with Alice's authority.

"I don't think 'detain' is quite the word we want here, Miss Wright. But I'm willing to take certain risks here, and once I have my promises from the three of you," he nodded his head around the table, "then maybe you'll understand."

Although he doubted it. He didn't think Alice Wright was given to a lot of understanding, and O'Herlihy was just an idiot. His hopes were pinned on Phillips. If he directed his conversation toward him, he might have an ally here. Damn, this was so uncomfortable. Frank hadn't always been the best cop in the world, but, by and large, he was an honest man, and hated this kind of waffling around.

He looked directly at Phillips. "What about it?"

Phillips, of the four of them in the room, was the only one completely at ease. Watchful, but relaxed, he knew something out of the ordinary was about to go down, but he could wait and watch relaxed as well as tense, that was his philosophy. "Okay by me, Lieutenant."

Alice looked at him with contempt. Look at that big Uncle Tom sucking up to the white detective. He wasn't fooling her for a minute, but at this point, she wanted to hear what Frank had to say. It would be such a feather in her cap if she could catch this white detective in something.

"Well, all I can promise is that I'll listen."

"Miss Wright, you'll have to do better than that. I want your promise that you will not do a thing that you haven't discussed with me and another party I'm going to name."

"Det. O'Meara, I don't have to promise any such thing. I am the caseworker on this case. I have a master's degree in social work, and I know my business. I will not commit to a deal and deprive myself of choices before I know what the choices are."

Frank sighed. Inside his head he said to himself: Get the kid gloves out, Frankie boy. The kid gloves and the Vaseline. Somebody's about to take it in the ass.

"Miss Wright, in no way do I want to encroach on your authority. Nor would I ever ask you to shirk your duty. In fact, as I recall, you have always been one to do what should be done, no matter how distasteful. That takes guts, Miss Wright, and that's something I admire."

Alice Wright just looked at him, but something inside her relaxed, and Frank felt, rather than saw, the tension in her lessen. "I can promise you this much, Det. O'Meara: I will be as open-minded as I know how to be to any suggestions you might have to make about the disposition of this case, and I will certainly hear you out before making any decisions."

"Nobody could in fairness ask for more, Miss Wright," Frank said solemnly.

All his hopes rested with Phillips, now. Sean's eyes were glassy, and Frank was not at all sure that he even knew where he was.

Frank took a deep breath. "First of all, Jason's fine. He's in good hands, he's not dirty, he's not hungry, and he's not being abused, sexually or otherwise. The person who has him wants only the best for him, and has my personal assurances that that is what will happen." He looked directly at Alice Wright.

"Det. O'Meara, I know my job, and that is what I and the state want for Jason, too."

"Well, good, then, Miss Wright. We understand each other."

He looked around the table. Phillips was cleaning his nails with his pocketknife, but his posture indicated that Frank had his full attention. Sean looked like he was going to start drooling any minute.

"Right now, he's with Anna Lee McIntosh."

Phillips' head jerked right up in astonishment. Alice Wright looked puzzled. Sean gave no sign of having heard anything, although he smiled and nodded.

"Who is Anna Lee McIntosh, Det. O'Meara?" asked Alice Wright.

"Well, she's a homeless person."

Alice Wright started to rise out of her chair, a look of unmitigated distaste on her face. "You tried to extort promises, knowing full well that the child was with an irresponsible..."

"Now, Miss Wright, sit down. There is no need for this. First of all, Anna Lee McIntosh is not, I repeat, not, irresponsible. Sgt. Phillips, will you bear me out on this?"

"Yes, Lieutenant, I will. But I gotta tell you this is one truly amazing thing you're tellin' us."

Frank softly chuckled, and said, "I'm sure it is, Sgt. Phillips. But I'll tell you the whole story in a minute. All I need right now from all of you is your assurance that you will listen and not go running out of here without understanding all of it. In fact, Miss Wright, this is the substance of your promise, is it not? An open mind or something to that effect, wasn't it?"

Alice's face was stony, but she knew she had been outmaneuvered. "Yes, it was. Please continue, Detective."

Frank looked at his hands, front and back, as he gathered his thoughts.

"I'm aware," he said, directing his gaze at Alice Wright, "of how unorthodox all this is. I know the rules and I generally like to play by them. However, at this point, there is no imminent danger, and I just wanted to be very sure of two things: first of all, that Anna Lee and anybody" (here he was thinking of Leon) "who might have helped her will not be punished. This is important. Their intentions were of the best. More people should be as kind as these people are."

"Just what other party is involved here, Det. O'Meara?" asked Alice Wright coldly.

"I'm getting to that, Miss Wright. But first, as I said, I want your promise that no charges will be brought against these people. Do I have that?"

Alice looked at him for a minute, then nodded. Phillips acquiesced with a short nod; Sean was nodding off.

"Okay, then, for thing number two: I will be personally assured that this boy is not going back to an environment that is not healthy for him."

Here he looked at Alice Wright again, and this time, his gaze was hard and unflinching. "Miss Wright, I'm sure you're not guilty of this, but too many times I've had to pick up people whose battered children died in the emergency rooms of hospitals, only to find out that the state sent them back after they'd been taken out. I dunno what kind of fluke causes that, but, by God, I promised Anna Lee this wouldn't happen, and it won't. Or, more to the point, if it does, I'll sure as hell get an accounting from somebody for it."

Alice returned his gaze, just as hard, just as unflinching. If anybody knew their job, Alice Wright did, and she didn't need some fool of a white man telling it to her. If he was so interested in battered children, where the hell was he when Effie was leaving bleeding welts on her back? She immediately repressed that last thought and reminded herself that she only did what was best for everybody, she knew what was best for everybody, and didn't she have degrees to prove it?

"I think I know what to do, Det. O'Meara," she said coldly.

"I'm quite sure that you do, Miss Wright. What I want is your assurance that it will be done."

"We always have the child's best interest as the focus of any case."

"Then you will do some thorough investigating before he goes back?"

"My investigations are never less than thorough, Det. O'Meara," she said haughtily.

"And where will he be kept while this investigation is going on?"

"Really, Det. O'Meara," Alice said indignantly, "I think this is a little too much. You're just going to have to trust me."

"Okay, Miss Wright, then let's put it this way. I will find out where he is put, and I will be on top of it at all times. Do we understand each other?"

Alice Wright nodded stonily.

"Okay, then, I'm going to call the place where he is, and then, as soon as it can be arranged, we're all going to drive over there together and pick him up. After that, I'm going with you, Miss Wright to talk to his mother. There is no rule that forbids this, and I'm going."

At this point Phillips, who had been absolutely fascinated with the exchange between Frank and Alice, interrupted. He knew Frank, knew him for a good cop and a good man. Also, he had seen Alice Wright around, talking to the juvenile officers, but hadn't really been able to get a line on her. This was the first time he had seen her in action. He was stupefied by the anger she kept locked away in her.

"Frank, I've been to the boy's home. The stepfather - I think he was the mother's common-law husband - is gone. Mrs. Anglethwaite says she put him out for good the morning after Jason ran away. She really seems sorry about all this and worried about the boy."

"Well, Sgt. Phillips, the permanence of the stepfather's absence remains to be seen. I've seen women in love do crazier things. I mean to keep my promise to Anna Lee."

Chapter Eleven

DAY FIVE, February 2nd Leon hung up the phone and went to the dining room. The building had been an old factory sturdily built of brick. As such, the windows were tall, letting in the morning light. It streamed down on to the old floorboards, picking up all the flaws that time had left, but making them beautiful with its brilliance. All morning Anna Lee had been in there, playing the piano and showing Jason some things that she knew about music. At first, she had been a little rusty, but after a while her memory, like that of a bicycle rider, returned, and she was playing and lost in another world, as the music flowed from her fingertips.

Jason sat there, enthralled. Once, when Leon tiptoed in, he looked up and whispered, "Wow! I didn't know she could do that."

Leon had smiled and answered softly, "I'll bet there's a lot about Anna Lee you don't know. She was once a famous lady, famous around these parts, anyway, for her way with a piano. She was young and beautiful, I have seen the pictures. Det. O'Meara, remember him in the kitchen yesterday morning? He used to go hear her play years ago, and he kept some of the reviews from the newspapers. She was really something in her time."

Now Leon was going to tell them that Frank had called and he and the social worker and two uniforms were on their way. The thrust of the conversation was that Frank had spoken with Lorraine Anglethwaite and, although it was by telephone, he felt reassured by her response that she really wanted her boy back, missed him, and it was her intent to make a better home for him. Frank let her know that he would be around periodically, and if he caught Billy there, there would be trouble. To his great surprise, Lorraine's response was a grateful, "Thank you, I hope so. Billy's a handful when he's been drinkin', and I'm just done with all that." Frank believed her (at least for now).

Frank had been as good as his word: there would be no trouble for him or Anna Lee, and Frank said he would personally see to Jason's safety in his home. He said that one of the uniforms, a Sgt. Phillips, had reassured him that Billy was gone, and that Lorraine was anxiously awaiting the return of her boy. After Frank's conversation with Lorraine, Alice Wright had gotten on the phone. Watching Frank covertly as she talked to Lorraine, she was hoping he would see what a professional she was, how neatly she handled these situations.

Alice and Frank had gone in Frank's car,

while Phillips drove himself and Sean in their squad car. They were now pulling up in front of the mission. Frank looked around for a parking place; failing to find one, he drove up the alley, and parked by the dumpster in back; Wilson Phillips followed. Everybody went in by the kitchen. Alice made sure that her little crown was straight on her head, and they went inside.

The first thing she did was look around and then say, "Where's the boy?"

Just then Leon came in, his gracious manner and warm smile reassuring to everyone. Frank thought: leave it to Leon; he's got social graces they haven't even invented yet. He ushered them into his office, bringing in chairs from the dining room. He pulled up one for Alice, took her coat and helped her into the chair like visiting royalty.

"Please, sit down. I wish it were more elegant, but you know, here we have to make do. Just pretend you're in a palace." He smiled, looking directly into her eyes, and hers fell in confusion.

Sean, who hadn't spoken a syllable since he'd come into their company, fell into a pile on the couch. He really needed a drink badly, but he couldn't let on. Furthermore, he didn't want anybody to know how very alert he was. He was just watching, waiting for somebody to try something. What was this bullshit, anyway, making promises to homeless dirtbags? He and O'Meara and Phillips were supposed to be cops. Was he the only one that remembered? He was ready, but he didn't want them to know it.

Phillips remained standing at the door, leaning against the jamb, and Frank just stood there in the room.

"Well, Leon, I guess we gotta take the boy now."

Leon said, "Let them say their goodbyes, Frank. It won't take but a minute. They're both ready for the separation, and I think they want to talk about maybe seeing each other again sometime."

Frank shrugged. Whether or not that would actually come to pass was anybody's guess, but the words had to be said, assurances made that no one would be forgotten.

In short order, Jason came into the office, looked at everybody and finally Leon, and said, "Okay, I'm ready."

He was clearly very shaky, and it wouldn't have taken much to start the waterworks flowing. But his slender back was straight and his chin high. Alice buttoned his jacket up to the neck, and they all started out into the little courtyard in back.

They were just getting into the car, when

Anna Lee burst through the door at top speed, her right hand in one of those roomy pockets, pulling something out. Sean Patrick O'Herlihy pulled out his weapon at a speed which exceeded that of light. When the bullet he fired connected with Anna Lee's great and noble heart, that organ exploded into smithereens. She was dead before her knees touched the concrete.

Still dazed at the unexpected accuracy of his shot (surely a sign from Providence), he was completely unprepared when Frank O'Meara flung himself onto Sean screaming, "You cocksucker! You cocksucking cocksucker!" and kneed him in the groin with all his might, simultaneously wrenching the weapon out of his hand.

Sean doubled over, spitting up stale beer, wet his trousers, and fell into a fetal position on the ground.

Leon was cradling Anna Lee's head on his knees, saying over and over, "Oh, no, Anna Lee, oh, no, Anna Lee." Finally he got enough of a grip on himself to reach into his pocket where he always kept a stole, kissed it, draped it around his neck, made the sign of the cross over her and began the prayers for the dying.

Alice Wright walked over and opened the fingers of Anna Lee's right hand. Jason's hat, which Anna Lee had conned out of the Rev. Joe

Reis, was crumpled up in it.

Jason looked up at Alice where she was standing with a puzzled looked on her face and said, touching the top of his head, "My hat. I forgot my hat."

Epilogue

Captain Louis Marcovicci sat quietly behind his desk, hands folded on top like a child in grade school. Sean Patrick O'Herlihy stood there, just as quietly but considerably more tense. He had just laid his badge on the captain's desk. The gun had already been turned in by that do-gooder suck-up scumbag who helped out criminals and attacked good police officers, Lt. Frank O'Meara. Sean was furious, but careful not to show it.

"You understand that IAD will have to have a complete investigation," said the captain quietly. Sean nodded dumbly. The captain kept looking at him.

Then he stood up and quietly swore at Sean. "You silly little sonuvabitch. I knew someday you were gonna cause me trouble. What the fuck is wrong with you, O'Herlihy? Don't you have the sense God gave simple vertebrates?"

Sean wasn't sure what a vertebrate was, simple or otherwise, but he'd had just about enough. The red flush began at his collar and spread to his face.

"With all due respect, sir," Sean began carefully, "I did the best I could under very trying circumstances."

"Trying circumstances, O'Herlihy, **TRYING** circumstances? I'll tell you what trying circumstances are. Trying circumstances are having the mayor's office call your home in the middle of the night wanting to know what's wrong with one of my officers that he has to shoot down in broad daylight an unarmed homeless black woman the same age as the mayor's maiden aunt. Trying circumstances is having the fucking NAACP picketing outside my office window, screaming for my head right along with yours. What could be more trying than that, Patrolman O'Herlihy? Huh? Enlighten me, if you please."

Sean just stood there and looked at him. He just couldn't understand what had gone wrong. His plan had been perfect. He would catch some felon, do some heroic thing, get the recognition and promotion he deserved. When his chance came, he took it. How he had misjudged the situation baffled him completely. All he had seen was a black woman the approximate size and speed of an Alaskan grizzly coming down on them in the back of Father Leon's mission; she was reaching into her pocket for God-knows-what, eyes wild, and Sean's instinct was not to take any chances. He had, in his judgment, responded rationally and speedily. He could not understand Frank O'Meara's reaction, which was to damn near make a eunuch out of him by kneeing him in the balls. Now he was facing censure, investigation, and probably the loss of his job. What the hell had gone wrong?

He continued standing silently, painfully aware that this interview was being aggravated by the fact that he desperately needed the drink that he had forgone preparatory to this interview with his captain. He didn't think that the odor of liquor would do him any good here today, but he could feel the shakes coming, and prayed he could get out of Marcovicci's office before they overtook him.

Marcovicci looked at him a second or two longer, then he reached into a bottom desk drawer and pulled out a thick, hardcover book bound in dark blue. Sean, through his discomfort, could make out two large A's embossed on the front cover. He slid it across the desk toward Sean.

"This book is called by the fellowship of AA 'The Big Book'. This is for people like us, Sean, you and me. Yeah, I'm AA, I have been for seventeen years, and I know a drunk when I see one. Now is as good a time as any for you to get sober and become a civilized human being."

Get sober? What the hell was the captain talkin' about? He was sober. Wasn't he standin' here, spittin' cotton and dry as the Mojave? Sean was flabbergasted. Drunk? What drunk? Sean could not possibly be an **ALCOHOLIC**. He just liked to have some fun once in a while, and knew how to do it. Alcoholics were like Anna Lee, whom he had shot dead, and no great loss to the world, either. He didn't rummage in dumpsters, stagger around on the street and live in gutters. He was Sean Patrick O'Herlihy, gendarme extraordinaire, and he had never missed a day's work due to drinking. The captain and others failed to perceive and appreciate this fact. They were just jealous; they'd do anything to keep him down.

"Don't stand there and look so surprised, O'Herlihy," the captain growled. "An' don't give me any shit about how you can stop drinkin' anytime you want. I used to stop drinkin' five times a day. Stoppin' isn't the problem; it's **STAYIN'** stopped. You've lost your wife, your job," Sean's head snapped up. "Yeah, I said your job. Now, I can go to bat for you to keep you out of prison, and I will, if you start going to meetings and make a commitment to stop drinkin'. If you don't, I'll pull the plug on you myself. I can't save your job, Sean," he continued softly. "But I can and will help you through the rough times. So will everybody in AA. That's what we're here for, that's what we do."

He leaned back a little in his chair, relaxing somewhat. "Look, Sean, I don't mean to lecture you. I know how you feel, I was just like you. I look at you and see myself. I've known for years that you have a serious alcohol problem. You're drinkin' in the mornings, now, aren't you? To keep the shakes away?"

Sean nodded, unable to move his lips. The captain sighed. Then he got up and walked around his desk, planting one hip on it and looking at Sean.

"Son, I know where it hurts and I know how badly it hurts. I'm offerin' you a way out, you don't have to be an asshole all your life. If I were you, I'd RUN, not walk to the nearest meeting."

Which is exactly what Sean Patrick O'Herlihy did. At first, he didn't know what to do. He had to acknowledge that drinking was no longer that much fun, it was just that that was all he had. If he gave that up, then he had nothing, he was in free fall.

It took a good while, but in about five years, he was living an orderly life, seeing his son on a regular basis (now an adolescent), even speaking to his ex-wife, who had remarried. He would never be a policeman again, but he had taken some courses in computer programming, and was building a new career. It wasn't always easy, and the dear Lord knew, it wasn't always fun, but, little by little, it replaced his old life, old memories, with a new life and new memories, and he was grateful. He was one of the lucky ones who never relapsed into the old habits. He had to walk a narrow path, never deviating from his routine of meetings, work, prayer and twelfth-step projects. He was frequently miserable, especially when he had to dig around in his old psychological baggage and clean out that nasty little basement in his mind. But somehow, it worked. He was never quite sure how. He just knew that when he lived by the twelve steps, he had peace; when he didn't, chaos reigned. He didn't know what the relationship was, and, after a time, he ceased to care. It worked like a light switch. The button was pushed, the light came on, you didn't have to understand why, just enjoy the illumination.

About three years after Anna Lee McIntosh's death, Alice Wright was found dead in her apartment. She had somehow overdosed on sleeping pills; nobody ever knew if it was purposeful or accidental. Maybe she got tired of the movie of her childhood that ran in her head, and decided to drop the curtain on it permanently. Or perhaps she had built a tolerance to the medication and had to keep upping her intake. Then, one restless night, in a drugged stupor, not remembering how many she'd had, she simply over did it. That was all academic. What really mattered was that little Alice Wright slept peacefully at last.

Fred and Margaret Lewison retired, hopped into the Winnebago and toured the continental United States with their grandchildren in tow. After that, they took a long trip to Israel, visited the Holocaust monument, and saw all the things that mattered. It was a second honeymoon for them, and they brought back presents for their children, grandchildren and Jason and Dodie Anglethwaite, who were once again frequent guests in their home.

It was really fun now, because Jason was in St. John the Baptist High School, he had converted to Catholicism, and he and Fred would have these long, theological discussions that always ended inconclusively.

During these sessions, Margaret showed Dodie (who was still the best reader in her school) the great literature that had come out of European Jewry: the folktales, Singer, Aleichem, and the more modern writers like the great American storyteller, Herman Wouk. Dodie ate it all up with a spoon.

Lorraine Anglethwaite had taken a very hard look at her life. She was not an educated woman, but she was by no means a stupid one, either. While working days at the factory (she hadn't lost her job, she was too good a worker), she started taking courses at night at Forest Park Junior College. A lot of midnight oil was burnt, a lot of salt sweated, but she got an Associate's Degree as a medical technician, specializing in blood analysis. She had been working in her career for about a year and a half now, well-paid and satisfied. She was even getting ready to buy her first home. She already had a new car. She could afford the tuition for Jason at a Catholic high school. Life was pretty good.

Two days after Anna Lee McIntosh's death, Frank received a call from the doctor. It was terrible news: he had prostate cancer. The treatment options were almost as bad as the disease, but Frank decided to go through with the surgery. It gave him an additional three years of life.

During that three-year period, he also decided that maybe Leon was right, he ought to lay off the scotch. He white-knuckled a couple of nights, and then found that it wasn't so bad, he could take it or leave it. He mostly drank coffee and soda now, all of it caffeine free.

This meant that Leon, likewise, had to change some of his ways. The big coffee urn now only produced caffeine-free coffee. Leon complained continuously about this, rolling his eyes with exaggerated martyrdom.

Frank retired from the Force, and began helping Leon at the mission. He even started getting some feel for the satisfaction that Leon had tried to explain to him. During the last five months of his life, Frank gave up his apartment and moved into the mission, still working with Leon's "guests" until he no longer could. Leon nursed him through those last weeks of pain as tenderly and diligently as a mother with a sick child, even though he frequently looked at Frank through a film of tears. When the time came, he administered the last sacraments, then lovingly drew the sheet over Frank's face, grateful that Frank's pain was over, but, oh, so very sorry that he was now left alone with his.

One April day three years after Frank's death, Leon was once again on his way to Calvary Cemetery, where both Frank and Anna Lee had been interred. Leon had seen to both, having said both funeral masses, and taken care of all necessary arrangements out of his small fund for the mission.

As he drove, he was once again contemplating the little mystery that had been playing itself out at Anna Lee's grave for almost a year now: somebody besides Leon was leaving little flowers and decorations on it. Who it could have been was quite beyond him. Her grave and Frank's were some distance apart, but Leon kept them both up, and when he did one, he always did the other. He would come up about every six weeks, and, even though the cemetery gave perpetual care to the plots, he liked to do a little weeding. He would bless both graves, and sometimes sit and talk to Frank.

One day some months prior, he had come up to do his little routine, and he noticed that Anna Lee's grave was clean as a whistle, nothing but beautiful, golf course quality grass growing on it. He was puzzled, but laid his little decoration down, prayed over it, and moved on to Frank's. Then he began to find flowers and decorations that he hadn't put down.

He was ruminating on this little enigma as he parked his car under one of the old shade trees in the cemetery. He looked across to Anna Lee's grave, some little distance away, and saw a tall, slender blond-haired boy sitting with his back to the drive. At first Leon couldn't tell if the lad was by Anna Lee's grave or somebody else's. But as he drew nearer, he saw that, yes, it was

Anna Lee's. He came up behind him, not attempting to be quiet, and the young man turned around.

Leon stopped in his tracks. "Jason. Is that you, Jason Anglethwaite?"

Jason looked surprised, then smiled broadly. At that moment, Leon realized that during those several days the twelve-year-old boy had spent at the mission, Leon had never seen him smile. What a pity; he had a splendid smile indeed.

"Father Leon, it's good to see you." Jason rose and extended his hand. He was eye to eye with Leon, who was a tall man himself, although now a little stooped.

Leon stepped back and said, "Let me look at you, boy. What a sight you are!" Shaking hands with Jason, he clapped him on the back with his other hand. "Tell me about yourself, what have you been doing?"

They both sat down, and Jason said, "Well, I'm graduating from St. John Baptist High School in about a week, and then in the fall I'm headed for UMSL, their pre-law program."

"Wonderful, my boy," declared Leon enthusiastically. "I didn't know you were Catholic."

"Well, actually, Father, I wasn't," Jason grinned sheepishly. "I think that you and Anna

Lee left such an impression on me, and I dunno, I guess it was a way of hanging on to her for a little while. I don't know why, I just associated her with the Church, and I felt like somehow I was keeping her close to me."

"Well, actually, Jason, Anna Lee was a Baptist. We never had occasion to discuss the issue of religion, but she got a Catholic burial. I'm the responsible party. I hope that from her place in heaven she isn't angry with me, but it's the only way I am able to do things.

"So, are you the mysterious person who's been taking care of the grave with me?"

Again he grinned sheepishly, and nodded his head. "Yeah, I got a car now. I'm eighteen, and I can drive, and this was one of the first places I came in it."

He looked up, shyly proud of the three great accomplishments of being eighteen, the owner of an auto, and having a valid operator's license.

Leon once again clapped his back. "And, so, it's pre-law, huh? Then where to law school?"

"Well, if I work my tail off, I can probably get into St. Louis U.'s law school. I'll probably need scholarships, loans and grants, but, what the heck, what else would I do with the time?" he grinned

"You could do a lot worse. And your mother and your little sister, they are well?" Leon had never met either one, but, of course, he knew of them.

Jason unfolded his lanky body and stood up. They started strolling in the direction of the drive.

He said, "Oh, geez, Father, you should see Dodie. She's almost fourteen now and really a looker. I'm already having to screen the guys who want to hang around." He turned his head around and faced Leon. "And that's almost a full time job, there are so many of them."

Leon laughed and threw a companionable arm across Jason's bony young shoulders.

Then he stopped abruptly on the walk, and turned and looked at Jason. "Tell me, Jason, do you know how to play chess?"

"Nossir, I don't."

Leon grinned. "Well, my boy, how would you like to learn?"

THE END